HoloCity Hard Boys

HoloCity Case Files #2

S.C. Jensen

Northern Edge Publishing

First e-book edition: December 2021

First print edition: May 2022

ISBN 978-1-990306-12-9

Northern Edge Publishing

Hague, Saskatchewan, Canada

Cover design by Martin — Cover Art Studio

www.coverartstudio.com

www.scjensen.com

Contents

Chapter One

I EMERGED FROM THE glaring lights of the legal theatre into a dim cement corridor. Hours of my own voice echoing off the dirty white walls of the witness box had numbed my brain. Now my footsteps echoed hollowly around me, and an emptiness rushed into my chest where I should have felt relief.

My testimony had been good. Councillor West would go down for the killing of Mayor Alice Randall. Even our corrupt legal system couldn't get past two eye-witness testimonies and the security cam footage from Randall's office.

Heavy John Harding hadn't piped up in defence of his high-brow henchman. He'd sat through the proceedings with a dull look on his fat face until the very end. West had spat on the camera and cursed his name. On his own screen, Harding had smiled like he liked it. That smile on the static-laced live-feed had crept its way into my mood like a poison. I couldn't shake the feeling that he'd been smiling at me.

But that was impossible. I was a secret witness. My audio and video were scrambled, and no one knew which courthouse I was testifying from. I rubbed the back of my neck with my flesh hand and rolled my shoulders, clenching the metallic fist of my prosthetic upgrade at my side. The janky skeletal limb pinched and twisted at the flesh underneath. I couldn't wait to get home and take the thing off. I flicked through my tattler, checked the credit situation and decided to splurge on a hack ride back to the Grit District, maybe grab some take-out on the way.

I leaned the upgrade against the outside door and pushed my way out of the building into a deluge of pouring rain. After a gruelling testimony under hot white spotlights, the damp evening air was a refreshing kiss against my skin. But as I stepped outside, an explosion of coloured lights hit my retinas like a nuclear blast and angry shouting drilled into my skull. Spotlights circled and cameras flashed.

"It's her," someone said, screaming to be heard over the commotion, and a throng of hungry faces rushed toward me. So much for flying under the radar.

News reelers swarmed the virtual courthouse like sharks frenzied over the scent of blood in the water. A huge microphone covered in electric orange foam lunged at my face.

A woman, hidden behind the orange ball, shouted, "Ms. Marlowe, Ms. Marlowe! Bizzy Bodies reel'zine wants to know, what did Councillor West do to you?"

"No comment." I shoved the mic out of my face with my metal hand. Three more coloured mics popped up to take its place.

"Is it true," a man's booming voice rose above the excited buzz, "that you invented this accusation as revenge against the man who refused your sexual advances?"

Someone else shouted, "Who really killed Mayor Randall?"

"No comment," I said, louder this time. I stumbled backward to get away from the surge of screaming reporters and back into the relative safety of the building.

I tripped over the door frame and scrambled inside, forcing the door closed in the face of the nearest reporter. Behind the coloured mics, the crowd swelled up the stairs of the courthouse. Palms slapped against the transparent concrete walls. Fists holding microphones pounded the door furiously. I yanked on the manual bar-lock with the upgrade until it sealed shut with a metallic click. There were no handles on the outside door. For the moment, I was safe. But the swell of voices outside grew more frenzied and I hit the emergency button. Security could deal with these gritsuckers.

But security didn't show. I cursed and backed away from the shuddering door.

The Biz District's Mayor, Alice Randall, had been dead for less than forty-eight hours. I had known the sharks would be out, but a creeping sensation gnawed at my guts. It wasn't her blood they'd scented. It wasn't Councillor West's.

It was mine.

My testimony was supposed to be a secret. Somebody had sold me out.

I turned my back on the commotion at the door and followed the dim corridor deeper into the virtual legal centre. The building was a concrete hive of corridors and dingy old recording rooms, designed for discretion and anonymity. Behind the soundproofed walls, and double-thick security doors were highbinder politicians, billionaire business magnates, and crime lord king pins all vying for their own slice of HoloCity's corruption pie.

Court cases were tried virtually with attorneys, defendants, witnesses, and juries all streaming from different virtual legal centres around the city. Nobody was supposed to know where anybody else was, or when the case would be digitally assembled and broadcast to the feedreel networks. It was supposed to be secure. Still, there must have been another way out of the damned place.

I was probably the only one stupid enough to try waltzing out the front door.

I came to a T-junction and glanced both directions. The low red glow of an emergency exit light flickered to my right, so that's the way I turned. I shoved open the door and crashed into a brown-skinned woman with grey dreadlocks tied in a thick rope over her shoulder.

"Marlowe?" The woman's skin wrinkled around her eyes like cracked leather. "What are you doing here, you got a death wish?"

Doris Fairweather, HoloCity's D.A. for Biz District affairs, pressed her age-thinned lips together into a crinkled seam across her face.

"No more than usual," I said. I glanced up the metal-grating stairs behind her, my eyes aching at the bright artificial light inside the stairwell. "What do you mean?"

She pushed me back into the hallway and peered over my shoulder with her eyes glinting like shards of obsidian. "You should have been out of here hours ago."

The emergency door shushed closed with a hydraulic hiss. I crossed my arms. "I just got out of the witness box."

D.A. Fairweather frowned. She grabbed a cord of thick grey hair in a wizened brown hand and flipped the braid over her shoulder. She brought up an encrypted holoscreen on her tattler and scanned something that looked like a timetable written by an alien species. With the right implant it would be perfectly legible, but that kind of tech was above my pay grade. Besides, I didn't work for the city. She grunted something under her breath, closed the window, and sighed.

"Where's your escort?" she said.

"I'm a lowly private eye, Ms. Fairweather." I leaned on the handle of the emergency exit again. "We don't rate escorts."

She cursed. "Chief Swain swore he'd see to it personally."

"I'll bet he did just that." I grimaced and took a piece of chewing gum out of my jacket pocket. Swain would have liked to see my guts spread across the Grit District like party streamers. It was one of his tricks that separated me from my other arm, and he'd been bitter about his failure to kill me ever since. I stuck the gum in my mouth and chewed. An electric explosion of artificial sweeteners burst over my tongue. I said, "The angry mob outside is probably courtesy of his protection program. Do me a favour and don't do me any more favours like that."

"You've been outside?" she said, the skin around her eyes tightening again. Her left eyelid twitched. "They saw you?"

I told her about my run-in with the feedreelers and she cursed again, more colourfully.

"Come with me, then," she said. "Let's get you out of here."

Fairweather stalked down the hallway like a woman half her age, which could have been anywhere from thirty to a hundred and thirty depending on her benefits package. She held her narrow shoulders stiff and square, her hands balled into fists at her side. The long grey ropes of hair hung past her waist and swayed across her back with pendulum-like precision. I wouldn't want to be Swain next time he needed the goodwill of the D.A.'s office to grease his latest deal.

"I came when I got the summons," I said and I hustled to keep up. "How could I have been out of here hours ago?"

She led me back the way I'd come, back into the main hallway where hands still beat against the murkily translucent walls and voices shouted.

"I booked you for an early morning time slot to avoid this." She indicated the silhouetted rioters outside. "The request was signed, sealed, and approved weeks ago. Someone had to pull some strings to get you rescheduled at the last minute."

"I'm honoured they went to all that trouble," I said.

"You've made a lot of trouble for them."

I shrugged. "If we put West away, it'll be silky."

Fairweather stood in front of a slab of solid grey concrete just like every other slab of concrete that made up the walls of the corridor. She subvocalized a command into her tattler and the wall sank into the floor with a low, grinding sound that buzzed in my teeth. Beyond the door, warm yellow light flickered off the polished stone tiles covering the walls.

Fairweather grabbed me by the metal arm and shoved me into the tunnel.

"After you," she said. "I have to prime the exit sequence from this side."

I stumbled over the threshold and looked around at the low-ceilinged corridor. Globe-shaped chemical lanterns hung on either side of the walls at intervals of about twenty feet. Otherwise the passage was completely empty. A prickling sensation crept over the back of my neck. It was a nice place to get stuck with a knife if the old woman was a friend of Swain's. But it had been her case against West. If I had to trust someone, I guessed it might as well be her.

D.A. Fairweather jumped over the concrete door as it rose out of the floor and slid back into place with the same grating noise. She bumped into my shoulder and I flinched.

"Feeling jumpy?" she said. "You should be."

"Maybe I should have jumped before I got into that witness box."

For all the thick grey hair on her head, the district attorney's eyebrows and eyelashes had thinned to nothing. She wrinkled her bare brow ridges at me and shook her head. "You didn't know what you were signing up for? Come on, Marlowe. You're supposed to be a sharp tack."

Heavy John Harding's dead-eyed smile flashed through my mind's-eye and I shivered. I said, "Harding took the whole thing a little too well, don't you think?"

"Councillor Harding is a man with many connections." Her grey-haired head nodded. "Look, the jury believes you. Your testimony matches the video footage. We could be looking at an indictment before midnight if there's no interference. But if West takes this fall, it's not going to look good for Harding or his associates. You're going to want to tread carefully until this blows over."

"Don't put any men on me," I said, figuring where she was headed with this talk. I snapped the gum between my teeth. "I know the streets of this town pretty well. Your men aren't gonna stick close enough to do me any good."

Fairweather motioned for me to follow and we jogged down the eerily glowing corridor. I felt like I was inside an Old Earth pyramid or catacombs. Our footsteps bounced along ahead of us like an army announcing our presence. Fairweather said over her shoulder, "You couldn't even get out of this building without drawing attention to yourself."

"This ain't the streets," I said. "And I was set up."

She snorted and continued jogging. The corridor sloped downward and curved to the left. The curve tightened in on itself until we were on a corkscrew-like ramp leading far beneath the courthouse. Fairweather said, "How well do you know Councillor Harding?"

"I know he wasn't always a Councillor," I said. "Heavy John Harding headed up the Red Line gang for years before he made enough cush to buy his way into highbinder politics. He's a fixer, the guy you gotta see if you want to open up a card den or a skirt shop this side of the Grit."

"Right," Fairweather said, her breathing only slightly laboured. "You having the goods on West was a surprise to a lot of people. The cam footage could have gotten lost. But they didn't dare make a play for it with two secret witnesses."

"Who's the other guy?" I said. "Now the secret's out."

Fairweather shook her head. "I'm sorry your ID was leaked, but we have to protect our evidence at least until West goes down. We kept your testimony mum long enough to get a jump on him. We need to put West away."

"You said we'd probably get the indictment tonight," I said. "Silky, right?"

"Maybe," she said. "But Councillor Harding has been implicated, and he's not going to like that."

"I didn't point any fingers at Harding," I said. "As far as I'm concerned, once West is in the clink, we're done."

Fairweather stopped in front of a smooth, black door. She lifted her arm to her throat and said something I couldn't hear. The door slid silently into the wall and we stepped through into a vast underground carpark. The D.A. strode across the cavernous room with her heels clicking like the staccato report of distant gunfire. I expected her to have one of the sleekest new boiler-car models, all shiny black or silver. Instead, she opened the door of a dented rental hack with raw gunmetal grey body panels peeking through the chipped yellow paint.

Wordlessly, she pointed at the back seat and I crawled inside the car.

She slid in across from me and asked for the grid coordinates of my apartment. I gave her my office address just to be safe. She keyed the directions into the hack's control console. Then she leaned back in the seat and put her wrinkled brown hands over her face. She sighed. "There's no doubt in my mind that Councillor West shot Mayor Randall. I've watched the cam footage a thousand times. You saw it with your own eyes."

"But you don't think he was working alone," I said.

"Mayor Randall was giving Harding a pain in the credit stack with her crack down on gang activity in the grit," she said. "He's attempted to block her at every board vote since his election. Could be he got tired of losing. I'm not saying he had anything to do with it, but I'd keep an eye on him if I were you."

"I'm only one woman," I said, snapping the gum between my teeth. I grinned at the district attorney. "Heavy John Harding covers a lot of ground. But I'll do what I can."

The hack slipped onto the maglev track leading out of the parking lot, the electric engine running as smoothly and silently as the sleekest new model. Fairweather saw the expression on my face and smiled wearily back. "Custom job," she said. "Easier to avoid the press when you look like a nobody."

"Being a nobody wasn't enough to keep the bastards off of me," I said.

As the hack wound its way up through the parkade and into the rain, I gazed out the security windows at the Biz District. Shimmering glass towers rose into the low-hanging clouds and disappeared. Hologram advertisements, projected against every smooth surface, danced and flickered in the rain in a kaleidoscopic array of colours. I rubbed my flesh hand through my hair and tugged until tears came to my eyes.

Men like Chief Swain and Heavy John Harding were so used to pulling strings and having it work that they lashed out when their strings got tangled. I should have learned that lesson after Swain rigged my plasma rifle to blow because I refused to back off of a case he had his fingers in. I swallowed a lump in my throat. I'd have killed for a drink to wash away the dark thoughts, but that life was gone along with my arm and my job with the HoloCity Police Department.

I could only dream of being the kind of nobody that didn't have to worry about the Swains and the

Hardings and the feedreelers of the world. I balled up my metal fist and punched the leather seat. Outside, the glittering adverts smeared together through the haze of rain and the fog of my breath on the window.

"I appreciate the risk you've taken to give this testimony." D.A. Fairweather leaned forward in her seat and rested her elbows on her knees. Her dark eyes flashed in the leathery brown skin and a thick grey cord of hair slipped over her shoulder. She pushed it out of the way and pressed her lips together. She said, "I want you to know I'll be out of town for a couple of days, I'm leaving tonight if this indictment comes through."

"Thanks for the heads up." Bitterness tinged my words. "But I don't think I'll be following you."

"Be careful—if anything should happen to go wrong, see Bernie Howes, my chief investigator."

"Not likely," I said, "if he's on Swain's payroll."
She sniffed. "He's mine. You can trust him."
I said, "Sure."

"You're hard, Marlowe." She lowered her voice and pressed the palms of her hands together between her knees. "But don't be so hard that you forget you're flesh and blood."

I grinned at her, but there was no joy in it. "Most of me, anyway."

The car pulled up in front of my dingy grey office just inside the Grit District and Fairweather opened the door for me. She said, "Thanks, Marlowe. Good luck."

I stepped out into the rain and kicked the door closed without saying goodbye and the ratty-looking hack zipped back out onto the traffic grid. I stared up the second floor window above the faded red awning of the vacant suite in front of me.

The cracked glass was too grimy to see through. But the blinds were open just enough to show a shadow moving on the other side, a shadow backlit by the yellow glow of a light I knew I hadn't left on.

Somebody was waiting for me.

Chapter Two

I CREPT UP THE back stairs of the building, dodging a couple of pinches passed out in the vestibule. The cracked glass of the entryway let in a pool of scummy water, but the couple—locked in the impassioned embrace of a glow up—didn't seem to mind. A pair of electric red platform pumps had been kicked off in the corner. Beneath a piece of sodden cardboard, pulled up like a blanket, a bare foot with a cracked and blackened heel stuck out. It twitched. Hopefully I wouldn't have to call for stiff removal in the morning.

Not long ago, it might have been me sleeping off a night on the town in the stairwell of a third-rate office building. I didn't want that drink so badly anymore.

I gritted my teeth and climbed the crumbling stairs two at a time with my metal fist clenching and unclenching at my side. Above me, a dim grey light buzzed and flickered like it had a corroded connection. It was the sound of missed rent payments and empty beds with cold, dirty sheets. A lonely, familiar sound that carried the bitter taste of last-nights sick on the back of the tongue. I rolled my shoulders and pushed against the bar-lock on the door to the second floor.

Another dim light in the office corridor greeted me. The doors to the other offices were all closed, windows blackened. From the far end of the tunnel some over-zealous moaning suggested someone had stayed late with a PornoPop 'gram, maybe even a flesh and blood pro-skirt. A rectangle of warm yellow light spilled out of my office, halfway down the hallway. My door, with BUBBLES MARLOWE: PRIVATE DETECTIVE etched into the glass, was cracked slightly open.

I pressed my back against the wall and inched my way toward the hinged edge of the doorway. I kept my metal arm up as if I had a gun. I hadn't carried a gun since my "accident" with the plasma rifle, but it wouldn't hurt whoever was waiting for me to think I was packing heat. I considered stepping in front of the glass, to let the person inside see my shadow before I opened the door. I didn't fancy getting shot by a jumpy client.

Then again, whoever it was might not be a client. And putting a plug in me might just make their night.

Before I could decide what to do, a smooth, low mezzo-alto voice slid toward me through the cracked door. "Come on in, Marlowe," it said. "This is your place, ain't it?"

I recognized that voice. Pushing the door open with my hip, I kept my arm up just for appearances, but I relaxed when I saw the broad yellow shoulders sitting across from my desk. Lou Lemon swivelled in the guest chair, her cropped black hair swept neatly over the left side of her handsome face. She had a thick brown cigar stub clamped between her teeth and the sweet, heady scent of imported tobacco hovered in the air. The density of the haze told me she'd been waiting for a while.

"What's the smoke, Lou," I said. "I don't remember giving you a key."

She grinned at me, her square jaw bulged and her cheeks dimpled. She rolled the cigar from one side of her mouth to the other. She said, "What's a locked door between old friends."

I kicked the door closed behind me, shook the rain off my jacket, and hung it up on the coatrack. I reached a hand into the pocket and pulled out another piece of gum before I went around the desk and sat in the swivel chair.

"I don't mind," I said, peeling the silver wrapper from the gum slowly, "so long as it's you. I just thought I had a better lock."

Lou shrugged the padded shoulders of the yellow suit and spun a matching yellow fedora on her fist. A cobra-headed cane rested between her knees. She leaned back in the chair and watched me stick the gum in my mouth. She said, "You still doing business or you selling your soul to the city?"

"I'm still doing business, if there's any business for me to do."

She bit down on the cigar and the end jumped up and down, leaving a snaky trail of smoke hanging between us. She said, "I heard you mighta jumped ship."

I pushed the gum over my tongue, blew a thin bubble, and sucked it back in through my teeth with a snap. "Gotta be careful what doors you listen at these days," I said.

Lou plunked the hat down on the cane and pursed her lips over the cigar, her green eyes flashing. "I got a little something for you," she said. "If you're feelin' dry."

I pulled open the drawer of my desk and took out a can of NRG soda. "I'm always dry these days," I said. "I kind of like it."

"I heard you were off the sauce," she said. She folded her thick fingers together and wrapped them around her knees. "Good for you. The liquor market weeps."

"What have you got for me, Lou?" I drummed my metal fingers on the desk. "There hack fare in it? Or are you just here to blow smoke in my face."

Lou took the cigar stub between her thumb and forefinger and crushed it on the armrest of the guest chair, spilling ashes on the floor.

"I'm making a play at Cat's Cradle," she said. "Cimarro's place."

"Candy Cimarro?" I said. "I thought she was in the skirt shop business."

She spun the cane between her palms and the yellow hat seemed to float in the air in front of her. "Was."

"Cat's Cradle is the old-fashioned gambling den, isn't it?" I said, cracking the energy drink open and taking a long sip. "Your old racket."

She clenched her jaws together and her neck muscles bulged. Then she flashed her teeth in a grin. "Somethin' like it. Look, I think I'm gonna be lucky tonight. I'd like to have a broad with a rod on my back."

"If that's what you're looking for, you should ask Miss Candy," I said. "She probably still has connections."

Lou gave a dry chuckle and flashed her dimples at me again. "That's not what I meant and you know it."

"I don't do guns, Lou." I wiggled my metal fingers at her. "We don't get along so well anymore."

"You forget how?"

"I forgot how to like it."

She reached into the canary yellow suit revealing a heavily muscled chest beneath a sheer white tank top. She pulled out a small bore pistol with a narrow black barrel and dropped it on my desk with heavy thud. Then she reached back into her jacket and produced the thin silver cylinder of a silencer. She said, "I'm not asking you to like it."

I picked up the handgun with my metal hand and inspected it. Old-school gunpowder and lead variety, a well-maintained antique. She dropped a handful of slugs on my desk, too, and the leaned back in the chair, bouncing the foot crossed over her knee. Picking up the crushed cigar end, she stuck it between her teeth and chewed.

"Tell me about this play, Lou," I said. I watched her out of the corner of my eye and I screwed on the silencer.

"It's been three months since I closed up shop on my old den," she said. "I wasn't making the kind of cush it takes to stay open in this town.

HCPD been putting on the pressure since Mayor Randall's anti-gang bill passed. You know me, I ain't no gang banger. But it causes inflation."

"Cheaper to run your business in the Grit," I said. I loaded the pistol and sighted it against the back wall. "At least you only have to worry about one organization. That's gotta count for something."

Lou sneered. "Yeah, I been lining Heavy John Harding's pockets for long enough. The fat, bloodsuckin' sonofavetch."

"I thought Harding only dealt in the Biz District," I said. I frowned, wiped the gun off with my sleeve, and dropped it on the desk between us.

"The Red Line gang took over for the usual squad patrol just after I went under," Lou said. "But I could see who was behind the rate hike from a mile away. Heavy John's spillin' out of his suit."

I didn't say anything. I leaned back in my chair and sipped my drink and eyed the handsome woman across from me. Lou Lemon and I went way back. She'd gotten me out of a few messes I'd gotten myself into while drunk as a skunk and puking in the gutter. I at least owed her my ear.

Lou slapped her hand on the edge of the desk. Her green eyes glinted manically. "That's the laugh, though, Marlowe." She grinned. "Candy Cimarro bought a new wheel at an HCPD auction. I know Ainslo, Cimarro's head croupier, pretty well. It's one of the wheels they took off me when they shut me down. It's got bugs."

"And you figure you know them, but Miss Candy doesn't," I said. "Is that it? Why wouldn't Ainslo tell her about it."

Lou waved me away. "They have some history. Don't look a gift whore in the mouth."

"I think that's horse, Lou."

"What's the difference. You buy 'em, you ride 'em, they eat your creds for breakfast." The foot was bouncing faster now. "Look, Cimarro gets a nice crowd down there at the Cradle. Little dance floor, off-line games only, it's a nice place for the punters to relax, you know? It'll be busy tonight. I got it all lined up."

I looked away from Lou and around the room. It had mismatched bioplastic plank flooring in various shades of faux-wood. A coat rack my friend and part-time secretary, Dickie Roh, and I had pulled out of a dumpster. The dented metal desk and used holophone sat beneath the fogged window. Pink light from the rain-soaked neon lights outside spilled through the cracked slat blinds, casting stripes across my desk and Lou Lemon's face. I cracked the knuckles of my flesh hand against my upgrade. It wasn't like I couldn't use the cush.

I tossed my empty can at the recycling chute on the wall behind Lou's head. She leaned to the side to let the can past. The chute sensed the can coming and sucked it into the wall tube and out of my office.

I said, "I get it like this. You think you have that roulette wheel tamed and you expect to win enough money so that Cimarro will be mad at you.

You'd like to have some protection along. Me. I think you oughta have your skull examined."

"You gotta trust me, Marlowe," she said. "Any of the off-line game systems have a kind of rhythm to them. That's why most places don't use them any more. But the fact is, it ain't easy to tame a gambling machine. The nostalgic crowd will lose their shirts trying, and somebody like Candy Cimarro is happy to let them. But I know this wheel. I been on the back end. It's foolproof."

I took out my wad of gum and stuffed it back into the tinfoil wrapper and dropped it into the desk. Then I shrugged. "I don't know about that, Lou," I said. "I don't know enough about roulette. Sounds to me like you're a sucker for your own racket. Maybe I'm wrong, but that's not the point."

Lou's tense smile dropped from her lips. "What is?"

"I don't want to see you get hurt, Lou." I crossed my arms over my chest and spun to look out the window. Beads of rain ran in rivulets down the glass, fracturing the varicoloured lights outside into shooting stars. "I'm not much for bodyguarding. What if something goes wrong and you get put in a box? Or what if it all goes down smooth, but Cimarro gets her hooks in us? I operate on the level in the Grit, Lou. If I don't, I'm no better than the rest of them. This isn't my kind of job."

"I ain't lookin' for a partner." Lou stood. The padded shoulders of her suit and the muscles underneath gave her torso a masculine triangular shape. She picked the hat up off the top of the cane and dropped it over her cropped black hair. She said, "I just need somebody to spot me."

I sighed. "Don't go, Lou. I don't want you doing this alone."

"I'm not doing it alone," she said. "I got a fine piece of boy-flesh to play the wheel. Fiver Valiant. Use to be a feedreel star. He'll keep Cimarro and her goons off my back. We'll make out cushy. I just thought I'd tell you."

I was silent for a minute. I said, "You know I just got through telling a jury it was Councillor West who shot Mayor Randall a couple of days ago. I might not be a popular face in the Cradle."

Lou smiled faintly and wiped the back of her hand over her forehead, under the brim of the yellow hat. She said, "I don't know. West didn't have too many friends, did he?"

"Maybe not anymore," I said. "But it's his ex-friends I'm worried about. Miss Candy's got her veins pumped full of stims most of the time, what makes you think she'll have an eye for a little twist like Prince Valiant?"

Lou shrugged and twirled the cobra-headed cane beneath a thick finger. She turned and headed for the door. She left the pistol on the desk. I cursed under my breath.

"It was nice seein' you, Marlowe," Lou said with an affected drawl.

I waited until she had her hand wrapped around the doorknob and I said, "Aren't you forgetting something?"

She looked over her shoulder and her green eyes flashed over the pistol, and then onto me. Her cheeks dimpled. She said, "Am I?"

I punched the desk with my metal fist and said, "I'll swing by Cat's Cradle tonight if you have to have me. As an old friend. I don't want any money for it. You keep your twist in line. And for gritssake, don't pay any more attention to me than you have to."

Lou's green eyes dropped to the floor and the dimples softened. The corner of her lip twisted a little and she didn't quite look at me as she said, "Thanks, Marlowe. I'll be careful."

Her yellow shoulders slipped out the door and the clack of her cane echoed down the hallway.

I sat still at the desk, stroking the pistol with the tip of my upgrade and biting the inside of my cheek. I flicked on my tattler and scanned the headlines for news on the trial.

A navy-haired news anchor from one of the more reputable feeds stared at the holoscreen somberly. I tapped her image and enlarged it, turning down the volume on the other feeds. "BizDiz News, this is Ruby Blue reporting. If you've been plugged into the shocking murder of Mayor Alice Randall and the equally shocking criminal trial charging Councillor Sammy West with the crime, you'd better sit your self down. The indictment was just returned, mere moments ago, according to our sources, against Sammy West by the Biz District's Grand Jury. West is a well-known anti-regulations lobbyist who served on the Board of Directors with Mayor Randall for two years. The indictment, a shock to his friends and business partners, was based almost entirely upon the testimony—"

My tattler buzzed violently against my wrist, pausing the newsreel. I pushed the call through to the holophone on my desk and leaned back in my chair as D.A. Fairweather's furrowed brow materialized before me.

"Indictment returned," she said.

"I know," I said. "Ruby Blue is telling me all about it."

"The media spin is worse that I thought," Fairweather said. "Watch yourself, Marlowe. The speculation about Harding is coming in hot. He's not going to be a happy boy."

She said she was catching a flight to the Eastern Sprawl and suggested that I think about finding my own way out of town. I wished her a safe trip and killed the call and the reels. I sighed and picked up Lou's pistol off the desk, twirled it around my finger. Maybe the rod wasn't such a bad idea after all.

I called Dickie and left a message for him to meet me at the Cat's Cradle as soon as he could. Then I stood, grabbed a long black trench coat off the second-hand coat rack, and stuffed the pistol into the tactical webbing sewn inside. Lou Lemon might be a damned fool. But that wasn't going to stop me from being an even bigger one.

Chapter Three

IT WAS A GOOD crowd for the middle of the week. Cat's Cradle was a smoky, basement level den. Dim, coloured lights strobed and a stream of electronic music thudded in the background. The bassline was so loud that it stopped being music and felt instead like the arrhythmic heartbeat of some dying beast. Cheap nostalgia stims flooded out of the air ducts, creating a vague sense of comfort and an acidic tang on the soft palate.

The dance floor, with it's illuminated floor tiles flashing, had been mostly abandoned. A few drunks and pinches slumped against one another, swaying to a completely different beat than the thumping bass drilling into my brain. The rest of the punters had gathered around the tables, wheels, and analogue slot machines crammed into the other half of the basement room.

I ignored the wheels and pushed my way through the indifferent crowd toward the bar. An old man leaned on the service side, watching the action at the tables. I shouted over the din of the music to get his attention, "You got anything to eat in this joint?"

The man turned his dull brown eyes on me and cocked his head toward the gaming floor. "You catching any of this?"

"What's that?" I said, and spun lazily on the barstool. It wobbled beneath me like it wanted to toss me on the ground. "Somebody pickin' em tonight?"

"Playboy over there in the red get up," he nodded with his chin. "Must be playin' with fistfuls."

"He a house skirt?" I asked, just to keep him talking. "Looks like he might have come over with Miss Candy when she jumped ship on the skin joint."

He scoffed and made a show of cleaning out a glass with a dirty dish rag. He said, "Candy Cimarro's still got her skin in the skins, don't fool yourself about that."

"So you know him?" I said.

The man curled a thin lip over his yellowed teeth and eyed the young man at the roulette wheel. "I wouldn't mind gettin' to."

Lou's twist was dressed in a skin-tight suit of what looked like red licorice whips. The strands criss-crossed over his pale white skin like lash marks, causing his plump young flesh to bulge between them invitingly. His head was shaved down to glistening skin, except for a stripe of burgundy braided down the middle with a red gem stone sparkling at the nape of his neck. The boy tucked himself under Lou's shoulder as the wheel clacked around in circles. He bit his bottom lip and leaned forward, exposing the back of his trembling thighs as the wheel slowed and landed on black. The crowd shrieked and threw their hands in the air, and Fiver Valiant pressed himself into Lou's side and planted a kiss on her cheek. He left a lipstick smudge on her jawline. She let her hand fall to his waist and slide over his rounded buttocks.

I turned back to the bar.

"You don't play?" the old man said and set the smeared glass in front of me.

"Roulette?" I asked. "Or boys dressed in edible club-wear?"

His gaze jumped over my shoulder again and he licked his thin lips.

"I prefer cards," I said. "Gives me delusions of control. And men my own age for the same reason."

"I'm not judging," he said. "What can I get you?"

"So, you got anything to eat? I'm starving."

"Long day?" He pushed the glass out of the way and dropped a bowl of high-sodium protein chips in front of me. He leaned on the bar again and watched my face, his own expression carefully neutral. Could have been the old bartender stare. Could have been something else.

I popped a couple of the chips into my mouth and avoided the question. I could still see Lou's broad yellow shoulders reflected in the mirror behind the bar. I kept her in my peripheral vision as the boy spun the wheel again. I said, "You got an NRG soda?"

He cracked a can, poured the noxious green substance into the glass, and plunked a couple of frozen metal cubes into the bottom. Water was too cushy to waste on ice when you lived in the Grit. I nodded my thanks, let him scan my tattler for the creds, and took a sip. My eyeballs buzzed from the artificial energy stimulants.

Behind me, a clear, very polite voice rose above the hubbub of the crowd. "If you will just be patient, young sir. . . Miss Cimarro will be here in a moment."

A couple stumbled up to the bar and the old man sidled off to serve them. I slipped off the wobbly bar stool and made my way toward a waist-high metal railing that separated the bar area from the gaming floor. Two croupiers dressed in lean white suits with pink lapels stood near me with their heads together and their eyes sliding sideways at Lou's wheel. One leaned on a chip rake and stuck his jaw out at Fiver Valiant.

Up close, Valiant looked even younger than I'd thought. I hoped he'd had some kind of age reversal treatment rather than Lou being a baby snatcher, but it was hard to tell. The front of his licorice whip get up left even less to the imagination than the backside. His narrow white shoulder glistened with sweat and glitter beneath the old-fashioned incandescent lighting strung up above the tables. Lou's yellow suit shimmered with iridescent threads I hadn't noticed back at my office. She kept her arm tight around Fiver Valiant's waist and whispered in his ear. He pouted and stomped a high-heeled shoe. Lou pulled back slightly to put some distance between them and stared off into the crowd.

"Why don't you two mugs zip your traps and spin that wheel?" The boy shouted, slamming his thin, ring-covered hands on the top of the table. "You snatch those creds away fast enough when Lady Luck is looking your way, but you sure don't like to dish it out."

The crowd muttered, heads turning this way and that to discuss the scene with their neighbours. The tallest croupier, a man with artificially whitened hair and pure white lenses in his eyes that indicated he was equipped with tech scanners, cleared his throat and glanced over his shoulder.

The croupier with the rake bounced it up and down on his foot and smiled icily at the boy. "The table can't cover your bet, sir," he said. His words came out with calm precision, though his lips quivered slightly. "Ms. Cimarro, will perhaps—"

"Ms. Cimarro can eat my candied G-string, highpockets," the boy said, baring his teeth a little behind wet pink lips. "I've got your cush, baby. Don't you want to earn it back? You don't want to spin the wheel I could come up something else for you to play with. . ."

Lou Lemon winced and ran the back of her hand over her mouth. She put the hand on the boy's arm, her eyes burning a hole in the pile of holocred chips piled on the green felt table. She said something under her breath that I couldn't hear from where I was standing. It looked like, "Wait for Cimarro."

"To hell with that vetch," Valiant clawed at Lou's hand and she let go of his arm. "I'm hot, baby, and I wanna stay that way."

The pounding music from the dance floor stopped suddenly and the basement den filled with the unnatural silence of hundreds of people holding their collective breaths. A chime sounded from somewhere on the far side of the casino and two transparent doors slid open. Candy Cimarro appeared inside the elevator, flanked by two massive pieces of muscle-for-hire in sharp black suits.

The men wore mirrored shades despite the low light of the casino and I was willing to bet my week's meagre wages that they could see more through them than I could without. Lou's gun itched against my ribs where I'd tucked it inside my coat. The door scanners hadn't flagged the ancient handgun—they were looking for plasma rigs and computerized weapons—but these goons were probably wearing X-ray goggles. I shifted so that I had a couple extra bodies between us.

Ms. Cimarro strode down the half-stairs onto the gambling floor in a sheer pink evening gown, her pale blonde hair piled in intricate ringlets upon her head like the swirls of icing on a cupcake. She was all sweetness and light until you looked at the stone-cold expression carved onto her face like her flesh was dead marble.

Her heels clicked across the floor in the silence. The patrons shuffled out of her way before she got close so that the crowd opened and parted before her in a sea of sweaty meat. As she got closer, her dewy complexion became a glistening pallor. Her grey eyes were still and wet as if she was looking out from behind glass. Her face didn't move as she slid between the two croupiers and placed her manicured fingers on the table. Then she smiled as if she'd heard of a smile once and decided to try it out just this one time. When she spoke, her words fell like pellets of ice on the roulette table, bouncing in the quiet.

"Good evening, Mr. Valiant," she said. The frost of it sent shivers up my spine. "You must let me send one of my men with you when you go home. It would be a shame if any of that cush slipped through your pretty little fingers."

The boy narrowed his false-lashed eyes in her direction. "I ain't leaving, Candy. Not unless you're throwing me out."

Cimarro's expression didn't change—it was as if she were a mannequin and was speaking from another room. More likely she her veins were pumped so full of stims she was speaking from another dimension.

"No?" she said. "What would you like to do?"

The boy leaned over the table, his thin white arms trembling, and pushed the stack of transparent, multi-hued credit chips onto the table. "Bet the wad—pro skirt!"

I'd thought it was quiet before. Now it was like someone had pulled the plug on a VR simulator. The entire scene froze, still and silent, while Candy Cimarro stared straight ahead, not quite focussed on the boy. But not quite unseeing. Gravely, she lifted a hand and flicked her wrist. An encrypted holoscreen appeared before her. With a deft motion she moved un-readable glyphs across the screen. She closed it and nodded to the croupier with white eyes.

"One mil," she said, her voice as smooth as an ice-wine from the northern trade zones, and almost a toxic. "That's my limit, as always."

I nearly choked on my NRG. A million cred wasn't quiet enough to buy a city block in the Grit, but it could make a dent in one. More than enough to get shot for. The pistol seemed to burn under my coat now. What in the name of Grit District good times had I gotten myself into?

Cimarro's goons scanned the crowds like security drones on an auto-loop—back and forth, back and forth—never indicating they noticed a thing while probably mapping and storing every face in the room. Sweat broke out on my forehead and I held the can up to my face like I was inspecting the label.

The croupier put a bony hand on the wheel and looked to the boy. His white eyes couldn't be read, but his mouth twitched like a rat with a piece of meat in its claws that it knows it doesn't deserve.

The boy gripped the edge of the table, his eyes glittering, and said, "All in on red, baby. I'm hot. I can feel it."

His arms shook and his toes rocked against the pointed heels, twitching like a pinch on the come down. Strands of burgundy hair fuzzed around the edges of his braid and the red gemstone jostled precariously at the end like he'd been running his hands over it.

The croupier with the rake dragged the credit chips around the wheel at the centre of the table and stacked them neatly into ten grand stacks. When he was satisfied Valiant could match the house's bet, he nodded. The white-eyed croupier brushed a thin hand over each of his crisp white shoulders, placed his fingers on the wheel, and looked to Ms. Cimarro.

"This is just the two of us," she said, as if anyone else might be crazy enough to dive into the deep stuff.

Heads turned back to the wheel. The croupier ran his palm theatrically along the side of the spinner. There was a hiss as the crowd sucked in another breath. Then his wrist snapped, the wheel spun, and he flicked the ball in the opposite direction. The polished wooden wheel seemed to sparkle as the incandescent lights reflected off the metal deflectors and the ball skimmed along the track. The croupier withdrew his hands and crossed them over his chest in full view.

The boy's eyes shone and his wet lips parted as if waiting for a lover's kiss. Lou stood behind him with her shoulders stiff and her fingers spinning the rounded shape of the cobra-headed cane.

The ball dipped out of the track and clattered over the bright metal diamonds, kissing each deflector as it hopped and jumped beside the numbers. The wheel slowed and for a moment seemed almost to spin backward before it stopped with a dry click. The little white ball lay motionless atop red twenty-seven. I let out a thin breath through my nostrils and crushed the empty NRG can in my metal fist.

The croupier with the rake pushed the boy's chips back toward him. One of the big goons behind Cimarro presented a black case, loaded the chips inside and passed it wordlessly across the table.

Ms. Cimarro turned her expressionless face back toward the elevator and the gathered crowd parted for her once more. One goon followed her. The other motioned with his chin toward the exit. He said, "This way for the rest. You've played enough."

I tossed the empty NRG can into a recycling chute and slipped backwards into the crowd, keeping an eye on Lou's shiny yellow suit, and checked my tattler to see if I'd missed a ping from Dickie. Nothing. But Lou was coming out of the crowd at me with a shiny look in her eyes and I turned back toward the bar to wait for her.

Chapter Four

Lou stumbled through the crowd like she was already drinking from the cup of plenty and tripped her way up to the bar. A pretty little thing in shiny black short-shorts was clinging to the edge of the stool next to me with the tanned half-moons of his exposed butt-cheeks. Lou bowled him over and somehow managed to fall up into the seat. The pay-to-play boy let out an outraged squeal and stomped off. Lou slammed her palms on the bar and shouted, "Barkeep, I need something that'll strip the paint of an old horse."

"Don't you mean whore, Lou?" I said. Out of the corner of my eye I watched a fat highbinder with a pinstriped suit grab Boy Shorts by the arm, a kit full of injectibles was spread on the table before the man, and I wondered if that was what Lou had in mind.

The wrinkled bar tender sidled over to us like he'd heard crazier requests and poured Lou a test-tube full of bubbling white liquid that smoked and frothed on the bar. "This'll do the trick, but it's best not to read the fine print."

His eyes lingered on me a little too long before he crab-walked his way down to the other side of the bar.

"Maybe you shouldn't Lou," I said. "The night's not over."

Lou stuffed a cigar between her lips and lit it with a pocket burner before spinning on her stool toward me. She said, "It's over for me. Two mil, Marlowe. I can finally get out of this sad sack town and make a life for myself."

"That's a lot of cush," I said.

She tried to take a sip from the smoking test tube, but forgot about the stogie. I grabbed it from her lips before it fell and held it while she emptied the tube down her throat. She coughed and shook her thick jawed head and then snatched the cigar from my fingers. She sighed and laughed and drummed her hands on the table. She said, "You see anything wrong with it?"

"I don't know much about the wheel, Lou," I said. "But there was plenty wrong with your twist's manners."

Lou's glassy eyes sobered up for a moment like she was running the play by in her head. She said, "He was just amped up, is all."

"You takin' licorice boy with you when you go?" I said, resting my metal elbow on the bar. "I hope you didn't leave him alone with all those chips."

"Far as Cimarro's concerned he won 'em," Lou said. "I'm not allowed in the counting room. I'm gonna meet Fiver and the hard boys at the back door. Just needed to clear my head."

She swayed on the stool.

"Silky," I said. The pistol was glowing nice and hot now. "I don't suppose they're going to transfer those creds clean and simple?"

"We're gonna deposit them at the night bank before heading back to my place," she said. "They split it up into a bunch of smaller transfers, less likely to raise red flags, you know?"

The electronic thumping of the music shook the floor and the barstools and made my heart beat faster.

"Sure," I said. "And gives Miss Candy and whoever else wants to take a shot at you a nice fair chance."

Lou tapped the side of her cropped black head of hair. "That's what you're here for. We've got a private boiler car waiting for us, a slick emerald green unit. You make sure we get in the car, I'll take care of the rest."

"Don't go too fast," I said. "I might want to follow you."

I still had enough credits left for a hack ride if I had to, but I hoped Dickie would arrive in his own car. And I didn't trust Lou to stay on top of little Prince Valiant with all that cush on the line. She nodded her thick skull and slid off the stool about as gracefully as she'd gotten on. Then she reached up and stuffed a handful of credit chips into my coat pocket.

"Buy yourself a drink, Marlowe. On me," she said, and I watched her yellow shoulders jostle away into the crowd. I checked my tattler again and saw a ping with the word 'Outside' from Dickie. I breathed a sigh of relief.

When I looked back up I choked on it.

Candy Cimarro, with her confection-like curls and her dress dripping off her like pink glaze icing, pierced me with a gaze that was anything but sweet. She said, "You don't like my place."

"I'm having a fine time," I said, and I waved the bartender over for another NRG. I'd lost sight of Lou Lemon but I didn't dare turn to look for her.

"You're not here to play," she said. When the bar tender dropped a can in front of me, she waved him away before I'd paid for it.

I cracked the tab and took a sip. "Maybe I'm here for the company."

She tilted her expressionless face toward me and whispered, her breath tickling the side of my cheek. She said, "I think you're a dick."

"I can be." I grinned at her over the edge of the can. "But I'd rather be friends."

She gripped my flesh arm with long, cold fingers and her perfectly manicured nails dug into my skin. She hissed at me under her breath, but her face remained utterly, unsettlingly passive. "You don't have any friend here, detective."

She said the last word like it tasted of sewage. I pulled my arm out of her talons and crossed it over my metal one, leaning against the bar. The glassy look was fading from her eyes and I thought if I pushed her too hard the mask would break and I'd be picking pieces of her up off the floor.

I said, "Have I done something to offend you?"

She pointed a finger between my eyes and bared her teeth at me. The finger trembled slightly where it touched my forehead, but I got the message all right. She said, "Nobody likes a snitch."

"Maybe not," I said, and I slid off the barstool and out from under her finger. "They don't much like sore losers, either. Better go get yourself another dose before you get too choked up about it."

She blinked at me once, twice. Then she threw her head back and laughed with a sound like breaking glass. I backed away and slipped into the crowd before she could decide she was going to have me dealt with the old-fashioned way.

I pushed my way through the sweaty, glittered throngs of dancers and bleary-eyed gamblers, to the silver double doors that led up the dingy stairs and out into the parking lot. Outside, the rain had stopped, and the coloured lights of the Grit District shimmered over the wet pavement. Out on the grid, boiler cars zipped by like streaks of white and yellow. Tall columns of light pierced upward into the darkness like spears, marking the pick up and drop of locations for hack cabs.

I pushed my hair out of my eyes with my flesh hand and reached inside my coat with the metal one. I wrapped my fingers around the grip and shrugged my shoulders, trying to loosen up the spot that kept pinching me. I would have to see about having Rae refit it for me. She always seemed to know what to do with it.

"Heya, Bubs," a jolly voice chirped from the shadows. I turned to see Dickie Roh, dressed in a bespoke grey pinstripe suit and matching homburg hat styled after his favourite Old Earth detective novels, leaned up against the wall of the entryway. He said, "What's the smoke? I thought I'd missed you."

"Thanks for coming, Dickie," I said. "You got your car here?"

He nodded and I motioned him around the side of the building. Lou had said they were unloading out back and I wanted to make sure I hadn't missed them thanks to my enlightening conversation with Candy Cimarro.

"What are we doing?" Dickie whispered behind my shoulder.

"We're looking for an emerald green boiler," I said, pressing myself against the wall as a couple of people stumbled out of a side door toward the hack pick-ups. "Lou Lemon is here with some dolled up piece of attitude and she's carrying enough cush to make Heavy John Harding roll over and take notice."

"Aw, man." Dickie cursed under his breath. "We aren't playing? I wore my lucky underpants and everything."

"I thought you'd be excited to be on the case," I said.

Dickie's eyes bulged over his pudgy cheeks and his mouth fell open. "I'm on the case?"

"Sure," I said. "I need you to drive. We gotta find Lou's ride and follow her until she gets home safe and sound."

"Okay, yeah." He nodded enthusiastically. "Green boiler. Cushy."

I peeked around the corner of the building and let out a low groan. The lot behind Cat's Cradle was packed and stretched as far as I could see in both directions. The Grit District didn't have much use for parking lots in most cases, since most of its denizens—like me—could barely afford hack fare on a good day. Miss Candy looked to be pulling in traffic from all over HoloCity, and with this many private boilers her clientele had probably pissed on more credit chips than I'd ever have to my name. The trouble was, finding Lou in this festering cush puddle was going to be like finding a sober pinch in a back-alley powder party.

"Why don't you go get your car and do a couple of rounds of the parking lot," I said, "I'll go on foot. If you find the car, ping me your coordinates and I'll come find you."

Dickie stood up straighter and tugged down the brim of his hat. He said, "You got it, Bubs. You can count on me!"

He scurried back around the side of the building and I slunk around the corner toward the back doors, keeping myself to the shadows. I waited by the doors and pulled up the collar on my coat—something Dickie had lent to me for my first case as a private eye and which I'd hung onto because, well, a Grit skid doesn't turn her nose up at free threads—and wished I'd brought the hat that came with it. My pale pink hair was a bit too visible for stealth work. In the brightly lit parking lot I was going to stand out like a glow stick. I kept my eyes on the cars, hoping to see a flash of emerald green or iridescent yellow.

A thick fog crept in between the parked cars and the floodlights reflected off it creating an opaque blanket of fleece to hide behind. After the back door to the club failed to yield anything of interest, I slipped into the mist for a closer look at the boilers. I kept my metal hand inside my coat and walked soundlessly over the damp pavement, mentally counting off the cars as I went and trying to figure out the approximate net worth of Candy's clientele.

When I turned the corner around the third row of cars from the building I stopped rigidly.

A man's broad shouldered shape materialized out of the fog like a hunchbacked wraith. A gat the size of a hacked off anti-aircraft blaster hung out of his ham-fisted hand and dangled at his side. He was shorter than average, and stood very still with his muscular legs spread apart for balance and his considerable weight poised on the balls of his feet like a dancer—if you like to call the old knuckle-busting shuffle a dance. The fog swirled around him as if he were a statue, but I knew that kind of stillness.

I pulled my left hand out of my coat very slowly, my heart hammering in my temples like the throbbing bassline in the club. Was it one of Miss Candy's hard boys? My metal arm, despite its skeletal appearance and pinching fit, was steady as iron. The fog seemed to swallow all the sound around us, like it had oozed into my ear canals and expanded there. All I could hear was my own blood pounding in my head.

The man shifted slightly, dropping his left hand with the glowing ember of a cigarette in his fingers. He flicked it underneath a boiler and blew out a stream of smoke over his shoulder. I tensed and tightened my finger against the trigger.

A light crunch of gravel sounded behind me and I whirled my head. But I was far too late. There was a swish of air past my face and an explosion of light behind my eyes, and a vat of black paint I fell into and under and couldn't seem to find my way out of again.

Chapter Five

WHEN I CAME TO I was cold and wet and a team of dancing elephants had taken up residence inside my skull. The pain seemed to be concentrated somewhere above my right ear. I probed the spot and found a nice piece of sponge cake there instead of my head.

I'd been clobbered by something that probably had the same size and shape as the meat-hook holding the super-sized gat. Did he have a twin? I considered Candy Cimarro's black-suited slabs of muscle. Could have been one of them, but it wasn't like Miss Candy was the only one with the cush to hire oversized goons in this town. She certainly wasn't the only one who might want to use them to lay me flat.

I frantically searched my coat and the ground around me for my own rod, but it was nowhere to be seen. That rated. Easy come, easy go. I couldn't say I was too choked up about it. With her winnings, I didn't think Lou would hold it against me that I'd lost her gun. That is, so long as she hadn't lost her winnings.

I groaned and pushed myself to my feet. I was on an overgrown patch of dirt stuffed between the edge of the parking lot and the cracked kinetic sidewalk beside the traffic grid. The back of my pants and boots were covered in mud and worse. I'd been dragged out of the way, but not too far. I glanced down at my tattler to see if Dickie had pinged me and swore.

The comm device had been pried out of my metal arm with a screwdriver. It would take me months to be able to afford a new one. I supposed I should be grateful they'd left me the arm. Even janky rigs like mine were worth a nice stack of cred on the black market. My best friend, Rae Adesina, had scored this one for me from her cushy job at an R&D megacorp. Maybe she'd have a spare tattler I could rent as well.

I shook out my hands and looked around. The fog still swirled around, and the neon lights and holograms near the traffic grid made it glow in shades of pink and blue and yellow. I didn't know how long I'd been out, but I had a feeling I'd missed the action with Lou and the little licorice Prince. I stumbled my way out onto the sidewalk and was greeted by a cheerful HoloPop of a little girl with rosy cheeks and bright red pigtails.

"You look like you've had a hard day," the hologram chirped. "Why not join me and my friends in Mr. Vermillion's Play House? Only three blocks away, in the Red Zone—"

"Report Pop," I said, waving my hand in the little girl's face. "Underage solicitation."

The little girl vanished and a grown woman with the same features ran her hands over a sequined dress and picked up exactly where the girl had left off. "—in the Red Zone, where all your dreams and darkest desires can be made true. Fantasy financing is available for a low monthly rate of—"

"Go away," I said. "I don't have any creds."

The woman evaporated in a burst of coloured pixels and reformed as a solemn looking man with thick rimmed glasses and a tidy business suit. He brought up an unencrypted holoscreen displaying my personal finances.

"Need cush, fast?" the man asked, making a stern face at the pitiful numbers strewn across my various accounts. "YumPop Producers is looking for women of your age and body type to star in select niche interest reels. Contracts being at—"

"Enough," I shouted. "Permissions revoked. Cancel. Cancel. Cancel."

The HoloPop flickered through its pre-programmed selection of personalized advertisements until it finally fizzed out and left me alone, waiting to ambush the next passerby. I ran my flesh hand through my hair and tugged up the collar of the coat again. A chill settled over me from laying on the damp ground and my head ached worse than I could remember since my drinking days.

But something caught my eye across the street. Tucked into a dingy alleyway next to an all-night curry shop, a flash of emerald green peeked out from behind an over flowing dumpster.

I waited for a gap in the traffic and made an illegal dash across the grid. Anywhere else in HoloCity a move like that would have been a death sentence. In the Grit there were few enough boilers and hacks on the grid that if a person was careful they could jaywalk without getting smeared through to the underside of the mag-lev tracks. Usually.

I arrived on the far side of the grid and stood beneath a buzzing orange sign that read OTTO'S CURRIED POTATO. The window was smeared with grime and the flaky remains of reflective paint proclaiming specials from two months ago. A square of warm yellow light spilled onto the cracked sidewalk outside.

A skinny pinch had tucked himself under the window on a narrow strip of synthetic thinsulatation matting and slept with his face to the dirty concrete façade, his bony shoulder moving with the shuddering breaths of someone coming down off a high glow.

Inside, the restaurant was empty except for a young woman in a hooded jacket with her hands wrapped around a cup of coffee. I slunk into the alley and had a look at the shiny private boiler. Emerald green, just like Lou had said. It had to be her car. But where was she? And if someone had knocked her down and taken the money, why would they bother to hide the car?

I came around the corner and accidently walked into the gaze of the woman inside the curry shop, biting her lip and staring out into the night. She looked away too quickly for me to ignore her. I stepped over the skinny ankles of the pinch by the window and pushed the door open. A bell hung from the ceiling and chimed when the door hit it. I glanced up at it and saw a little black eye peeking out from a crack in the plaster of the wall. Looked like Otto'd had some trouble with robberies and hoped to have some law behind him in case he wanted to shoot someone in self-defence.

At the sound of the bell, a big black man emerged from the tattered sheet of plastic that separated the dining area from the back room. He had a few hairs left around his ears and the back of his head and the rest seemed to have migrated to the thick tuft bursting out of his shirt. He wore the multi-coloured button down shirt untucked over a pair of grease-stained grey slacks. He said, "You want food?"

I walked past the young woman at the table and sunk a hand into my pocket to check how many chips Lou had given me. I said, "How much for the special?"

"What special?" he said, shrugging his rounded shoulders. "We got curried potatoes or curried potatoes with fry-meat."

"Real meat?"

He crossed his arms over the psychedelic shirt. "You're in the Grit, sister, whaddaya think?"

"Real potatoes?"

"How the hell do I know?" he said. "I don't question the guy that delivers the things. I check 'em for roaches and rat droppings and I calls it silk. Now are you buyin' or am I kickin' your sorry behind onto the grid?"

"Gimme the special," I said. I motioned to the woman with my thumb. "And one for my friend there."

"Ain't nothin' special about it." The man pushed through the plastic, muttering under his breath.

I grabbed a chair from the only other table in the joint and swung it around so I could sit facing the hooded figure. I crossed my arms over the back of the chair and grinned at her. I said, "That your ride out there?"

She turned her head so I could only see her profile, a fine aquiline nose that looked like it had been broken once or twice. Smooth brown skin and the hint of a cleft lip.

"My cousin's," she said with a faint lisp.

"Care for a batch of Otto's finest?" I said. "May or may not be real meat and potatoes, but almost certainly no rat droppings."

When she didn't laugh, I added, "Your cousin is an old friend of mine."

She nodded slowly and swallowed too hard. Her fingernails tapped the empty ceramic coffee mug in front of her. Then she brought it to her mouth and flinched when she realized there was nothing in it. She set it back down and licked her lips.

I reached down and drummed my metal fingers on the chipped laminate surface of the table and said, "We don't have to do this the hard way, you know."

Her gaze flicked to me from under the hood and I caught the glint of transparent visilens glasses tucked into her dark hair beneath the hood. She said, "Wh-what's eatin' you then?"

There was a clatter from the kitchen and a loud string of colourful curse words. Then the wide, rainbow hued shoulders came backing out from behind the sheet of plastic and the big man spun with two steaming bowls of electric yellow stew ladled over white rice. He plunked them down on the table, then pulled two spoons out of his back pocket. He inspected them with a frown, fogged them up with his breath, and buffed them each on his shirt. Then he dropped a bottle of red sauce on the table between us, said, "Extra spicy," and walked back into the kitchen.

I grimaced and wiped the spoon on my own shirt before digging into the curry. The young woman just sat there. I said, "Aren't you hungry?"

"Hard to work up much of an appetite when you don't know if the person you're sitting across from you is going to put a hole in your head."

"Why would I do that?" I ate a few more spoonsful and added some of the red sauce to my bowl. I stirred it in slowly and said, "Maybe because, the broad whose car that is doesn't have any family to speak of? Cousins or otherwise."

The woman's shoulders stiffened and I got ready for her to run.

Chapter Six

T HE WOMAN TENSED LIKE she might make a break for it. Then she clenched her fists together and put them in her lap and leaned back in her chair. She gave me a hard look and said through clenched teeth, "You figure it's a hot car?"

"No."

"You don't think it's a hot car?"

"No. I just want the story," I said and licked the burning sauce off my lips. "I want to share it over Otto's Curried Potatoes. They're bloody delightful, if you want to know."

She picked up her spoon and held it in her fist like she might have to gouge my eyeballs out with it. She said, "You a cop?"

"Private eye," I said. "But this isn't a shakedown. I'm not all that interested in you. But that's my friend's car and I want to know why she's not in it."

She pulled back her hood and dropped the visilens glasses over her eyes and scanned my face. Long black hair fell out of the hood. She said, "You're Marlowe?"

"That's me," I said. "Nice trick."

"You used to be a cop," she said, narrowing her eyes at me.

I waved my metal hand at her and said, "I got retired. Chief Swain would rather I got dead."

Her dark eyelashes parted as her eyes went wide at something she saw on the visilens glasses. But the corner of her lip twitched upward and she said, "That rates. I could lose my job over this, but I needed the cush."

"Don't we all?"

"Your friend in the yellow didn't seem to be suffering any." She rubbed at the scar on her lip with a neatly trimmed fingernail. She said, "I'm a hack operator for one of those old-style rental services where they like you to pretend you're really driving the car. Got a funny little hat and bow tie and everything."

"You're not wearing it."

"That was part of the deal," she said, finally digging into the stew. She paused after the first bite and chewed thoughtfully. "Thought it was a bit strange, but you know these highbinders. They get off on that kind of thing. They like to feel like having enough cush makes you the king of the castle. But I did it, so I guess maybe it's true."

"What did you do?" I asked, scraping the bottom of my bowl out with the spoon. Then I licked the last of the sauce off the spoon and pushed them both aside.

"I dropped a fare at Cat's Cradle," she said, flipping the glasses back up into her hair. "Then this big broad in a shiny yellow jacket sidles up with a kid dressed in red strings and she says he wants to play at being a hack driver for the night. Baby gets what baby wants, or some pizzle like that. But she's got a stack of credits in her hands, a hard grand. I can't say no to that. I got a little boy at home, and I don't want him growing up to be some highbinder's rent-a-bottom, you know?"

I nodded and motioned for her to continue. She ate a few more mouthfuls as if suddenly realizing I hadn't been lying about the curry. It was top shelf.

"She said she'd leave my hack at the apartment stacks across the line." The woman wiped her lip again and made a spiralling gesture. "You know the one, with the glass and the eco-sculptures?"

I whistled under my breath. "The Spire?"

"That's it," the woman said. "She said to bring her car to the Spire and she'd give me another grand."

She pushed her bowl aside and stared at me defiantly. I said, "And what was her story?"

"Said she and her twist had had some luck at the tables and they were worried about holdups on the way back to the BizDiz. That rates with me. Always spotters watching the play."

"I can't poke any holes in it," I said. "You got ID?"

She tapped a button on the side of her visilenses and projected a photo license that named her as Velma DeLuce of Busy Bus Party Rentals. I moved to scan it with my tattler then remembered some jackalope had fried it for me. I'd just have to use the old wet-ware storage and try to remember that.

The big man banged out of the kitchen again and came back to clear our dishes. He said, "Real enough for you?"

"Real enough," I said, and pushed him a stack of credit chips.

He grunted and scooped the credits into the pocket of a half apron he had tied around his waist under the flamboyant shirt. Then he disappeared back into the kitchen.

"Well, Velma," I said. "Let's go get your hack. I don't think you should wait around here any longer with that green paint flashing in the alley."

She winced. "I thought it was hidden pretty well."

I waved at Otto's hidden camera, and ushered Velma out the door in front of me. She pulled her hood up and kept her head down as she stepped into the street and walked into a man coming through the door at the same time.

"Watch it," she grumbled.

"Sorry," a familiar voice said from beneath the grey brim of a homburg hat. Dickie's face popped out from behind Velma as he sidestepped out of her way. "Heya Bubs, I thought that was your 'do through the window. What are you doing in here? I've been looking all over for you."

"I had a little run in with a couple of knuckle-happy schmucks in the parking lot," I said, rubbing the side of my head with my flesh fingers.

"You should have pinged me," Dickie said. He lifted his arms and held his hands before him like deadly blades. "I coulda backed you up."

"I was too slow," I said and I showed him my tattler. "And then I was too late."

"Rotten luck, Bubs." Dickie dropped his arms and eyed the young woman next to me. Velma seemed to retreat even deeper into her hood. Dickie grinned, his round apple cheeks pushing up over his crescent-shaped eyes until they disappeared completely. He nudged me in the ribs and said, "Who's your friend?"

I clapped him on the shoulder and spun him around. "I need you to go back to the office, Dickie. Lou might try to get a hold of me there."

"What about the green boiler?" he said, turning back to face me. "I haven't seen it anywhere."

I bit the inside of my cheek to hide a smile and said, "We musta lost it, Dick. Thanks anyway."

He sighed and rubbed his forehead underneath the brim of his hat. He said, "If she calls, how am I going to get a hold of you?"

"I'll be along shortly," I said. "I just have to check something out first."

He kicked the toe of his highly polished two-toned shoe against the wall of the restaurant and frowned. "You're not mad at me?"

"I'm the one who got myself knocked on the head." I squeezed his shoulder. "I need you to wait at the office—"

"For the phone," he said, pouting a little. "Like a secretary. I want to be in on the action, Bubs!"

A rush of wind and lights shot past as a group of boilers sped over the grid, ruffling my hair and forcing Dickie to hold onto his hat. When it was over, Dickie raised his eyebrows at me hopefully.

I scowled. "If it makes you feel any better I could knock you on the head."

He jumped backward a couple of steps and gave me a sharp salute.

"That won't be necessary," he said. Then he brushed his lapels off, tipped his hat to me, and winked. "Secretary duty suits me just fine."

He walked off, shoulders slumped, to where his boiler was parked at the end of the block.

"See you soon," I shouted at his back. He waved without looking.

I felt a pang of guilt at cutting him out of the latest development, but as much as Dickie idolized the fictional detectives of his favourite feedreels, I didn't think he was cut out for what we might find at the Spire. Dickie was a Biz District kid, the disowned heir to a PornoPop empire with more wealth than a mid-sized trade zone. He may have lost his inheritance, but he still lived a sheltered life on a cushy allowance from his estranged parents. He had no idea what it was like to actually live and die by the rules of the Grit.

"Shall we?" Velma said from inside her hood.

She backed around the corner of the restaurant into the alley and I followed. She tapped the side of her visilenses and opened the door with a passcode Lou must have given her. A spherical lens whirled open on the side of the car, creating a round opening for us to enter the vehicle by. I slid inside first and Velma followed. Without another word, she manually steered the boiler around the overflowing dumpster and back out onto the maglev grid where it zipped into traffic like any other boiler.

Velma punched the coordinates for the Spire into the console and leaned back in the seat.

"So what's with this broad, Lou?" she said. "I thought the request was a little sideways."

"I'm hoping it's just like she said." I stared out the window at the glittering nighttime cityscape below as we rose up to the higher mag tracks reserved for longer distance travel. The Spire was a long ride from the Grit in every sense. "I'm hoping she wanted to dodge the spotters, and that she's safe and sound in her luxury suite in the Spire."

"You know many folks who can afford suites in the Spire?" she asked.

I smiled thinly and took out a piece of bubble gum from my pocket. I said, "Until you mentioned it, I didn't think I knew any."

Velma grunted something, then leaned her head back against the seat and closed her eyes. The thin scar of her cleft lip caught the light and cast a shadow that turned her soft mouth into something as hard and sharp as broken glass. I guessed Velma DeLuce was the kind of woman who could give a person a hard time if she wanted to. For now she didn't seem to want to, and I was grateful for that.

I chewed the gum in silence wishing the elephants dancing in my skull would take ten while I thought about things. Lou couldn't have afforded a place in the Spire before she'd made her play on Candy Cimarro's new wheel, so she must have planned on renting a unit from one of the hotel floors. If she made it to the Spire, she would probably be okay. Their security would be tough to crack. If she didn't, there wasn't any way I could help her. My tongue stuck to the top of my mouth as I considered that.

When we arrived at the Spire, though, Velma's cab was right where Lou had said she'd leave it. We both breathed a sigh of relief.

After she'd parked the emerald green boiler and double checked the Busy Bus hack was in one piece, she pulled back her hood and shook my hand.

"Does that fix me up, then?" she said. "Can I go now? I gotta get back to my boy."

"Hang tight a few minutes, if you don't mind," I said. "I'll see if I can rustle up that extra grand Lou owes you."

She pressed her lips together, but nodded. "I can wait a bit."

I left her in the hack, inspecting the uniform she'd leant to Lou's toyfriend. As I entered the lobby—the only room in the building the likes of me would ever see—an electronic voice greeted me.

"Welcome to the Spire," it said, and the glass doors of the vestibule slammed closed in my face. "You do not appear to have sufficient credit to proceed."

I hammered on the clear door and shouted at the host who was filing his nails behind the reception desk. He looked up with a bored expression on his face, pretending not to see me. Then he did a double take, his eyes bulging in his head, and he dropped the file. He blinked at me a couple of times and I pounded on the glass again. Then he slid out from behind the desk and took a dozen mincing footsteps toward me, while looking over his shoulder to make sure no one else was around. The long blue hair of his tinsel wig swayed back and forth behind him.

When he got to the other side of the glass he stared at me, but didn't open the door.

"You gonna let me in, buddy?" I said. "Or are you just here for the show?"

"It is you," he said, pressing his neatly trimmed fingernails together in a strange, closed fist prayer. "Isn't it? I thought I was seeing a ghost."

"Do I know you?" I glowered at him. He was the kind of man who had too much fashion and not enough sense. Unfortunately, he was also the kind of man who could keep me out of places I needed to get to. So I turned my frown upside down and attempted a smile.

"Me?" he gasped, and took a step back. "Oh no. But everyone knows you, Ms. Marlowe. I'm just surprised to see you so... alive."

His thin eyebrows, crafted from shiny blue-green sequins like fish scales, arched so far into his hairline I thought he was going to knock his wig off. Probably would have been an improvement.

I dropped the smile again. "What's that supposed to mean?"

"Well, the murder of course," he gushed, pressing his palms against the glass like he wished he could get close enough to touch me. "It was terribly brave of you to testify. I thought for sure they'd have composted you by now."

"Oh, that." I folded my arms across my chest. "Sorry to disappoint you. Could you let me in? I need your help."

He backed away from the glass again, his gaze darting around nervously. "I don't think that's a very great idea."

"Not that kind of help," I said. Somehow I managed to stop myself from rolling my eyes. I tried the smile again. It came out feeling as brittle as a boxed-dye bleach job. "I have a friend staying at the Spire. I need to get a message to her."

"You have a friend?" he said with a frown. "Here?"

This time I did roll my eyes. "Yes. There are a few people left in this city who don't want to kill me, and one of them is staying here. Lou Lemon. Could you check to see if she's in please?"

The sequined merman stared blankly at me for so long I thought I might have accidently fried one of his circuits, until I saw a flicker from his irises that told me he must be scanning the guest registry from transparent smart lenses or some kind of ocular implant. Eventually he said, "Lemon, yes. She's registered here. But she hasn't come in or out since I've been on shift."

"And how long ago was that?"

He smiled coyly and batted his eyelashes at me. "I get off at three."

Holoprojected waves washed over the walls behind him, glittering with sunlight recorded from another time and place. Phytoplankton-like orb lights carried by micro-drones, swayed drunkenly around the ceiling. I wondered if the merman get up was part of his uniform or if he actually liked looking like that.

"Thanks for the tip," I said. "But I might be hazardous to your health. Is that a twelve hour shift?"

The flirtatious spirit oozed out of him like someone stepped on a party balloon with their stilettos. He nodded.

"Would you call up for me, just in case?"

"I already did," he said. "No answer. Sorry."

I shrugged and turned away from the glass door that would never open for me. Over my shoulder I said, "Thanks."

I pulled up my collar and walked out to the lot. It was smaller than the one behind Cat's Cradle. Mostly underground, I assumed. It didn't take me long to notice the problem. I scanned the lot, the sidewalks, the street. Velma DeLuce and the Busy Bus rental hack were nowhere to be found.

Chapter Seven

I USED THE LAST of the credits Lou had stuffed into my pocket to hail a hack back to my apartment, where I expected a lecture from my sobriety support SmartPet about the importance of punctuality. It was programmed to give me a hard time when I didn't come home within a reasonable range of my projected schedule.

But when I opened the door, Mittens, the black and white simulated cat, arched its back and picked its way across the floor to greet me with its eyes half open. It said, "You're alive."

"Don't sound so pleased about it," I said, tossing my coat on the back of a ragged armchair next to the door.

"I'm glad." It purred and rubbed it's nanoparticle skin up against my pant legs. "The adoption request protocols in the case of sudden and unexpected deaths of SmartPet caretakers are a nightmare."

"You're glad. . ." I said. "Because you didn't want to have to do any paperwork?"

"I hate the word paperwork," it said. "So anachronistic."

"Says the robot dressed like an animal that's been domesticated for ten thousand years."

"You know," it said. "I kind of like it when you're not here."

"Next time we do an update I'm turning you into a dog."

I stomped into the kitchen and opened the dented icebox. A single can of NRG sat in the middle of the shelf. I reached for it, but the curried potatoes gurgled in my stomach and I had second thoughts. I closed the door and sank onto one of the hard plastic chairs of my dinette set.

"You smell like you've been on a bender." The cat sniffed around my feet disdainfully. "Except you forgot to drink."

"I didn't forget," I said. "I chose not to."

It sat on its haunches and curled its tail around its body, lifted a paw, and proceeded to groom its fake fur. "And how do you feel about that choice?"

"I'm not in the mood for a therapy session right now, Mittens." I poked at the tattler and wondered if I had any spare parts laying around that I might use to fix the thing. I showed it to the cat. "Can you help me repair this?"

"I could," it said, "if you were even remotely competent with electronics."

I huffed and resisted the urge to flick the stupid cat-bot between the eyes. "I could figure it out."

"You barely know how to turn your tattler on," Mittens said, closing its green eyes to thin slits as if it was an effort to continue speaking to me. "I'm surprised you even noticed it was broken."

"So can we fix it?"

It yawned, flashing long white fangs at me. "No."

"I can't access my accounts without it," I said. "Do we have any credit chips laying around? I need to get back to the office."

I told it briefly about the job with Lou Lemon and how it had gone sideways on me. The cat feigned disinterest, but I knew it couldn't help analyzing data.

"I'd have thought you'd want to lay low after that verdict." Mittens stretched its front legs forward, closed its eyes, and sank onto its belly. Then it rolled onto its back and cracked one eyelid open in my direction. "The feedreels have been frothing at the mouth. There are bets on how long it will take for Harding to pull your plug."

"Oh yeah?" I said. "How long are they giving me?"

It closed its eyes. "I've got long odds on you at thirty-six hours, plus."

"Gee, thanks." I stood up and rifled around the kitchen drawers for spare credits I might have left lying around. Finding nothing, I headed for the bedroom.

I changed out of my mud-streaked clothes and into a slightly rumpled ensemble I put together from the semi-clean laundry strewn around my room. In the pocket of the faded black cargo pants I discovered a partially used credit voucher a client had paid me with for a tail job I'd done last week.

A woman wanted to know where her teenaged son was sneaking off to every night, worried he was caught up in one of the black market tech gangs. I hated jobs like that. It was almost always bad news. But this time, I got to report back that her son had gotten a side job washing dishes at one of the hock market food carts. Kid wanted some kitsch upgrade and didn't want to ask his mom for the cush because he knew funds were tight. She was so relieved she cried. I tried to refuse payment, but she'd slipped the card into my pocket as I was leaving and I didn't have the heart to push it back at her. Pride is its own commodity among the poor. I knew that all too well.

But thinking of her made me wonder about Velma DeLuce. Why had she left me at the Spire? Maybe she'd clued into who I was and decided it wasn't worth the risk to be sharing a car with me. Maybe there was more to her story than she was letting on.

I stood in front of my cracked bedroom mirror and ran my fingers through my hair. It had about three days worth of styling wax in it. The recycled rainwater our building supplied was tightly rationed, and I tried to save half of what I got for backup in case there was a shortage. I added a bit of sparkly red lipstick and shrugged. Good enough for the Grit.

When I came out of the bedroom again, the SmartPet was "sleeping" on its charger in the living room. I flicked a balled up tinfoil gum wrapper at it and pulled on my coat. I said, "Aren't you going to say goodbye?"

"I thought your plan was not to die," it said without opening its eyes. "I have a substantial number of credits on it."

"I know. You hate paperwork."

"Don't disappoint me."

I rummaged around in the junk behind my door until I found the hat that matched the coat and crammed it onto my head. "How do you have credits, anyway? You're a household appliance."

"If you have to ask that question you'd better not look too closely at your credit statements."

I gritted my teeth. I'd placed every protection I could think of on accounts to keep the cat from spending my cush, but it always found some loophole in the contract regarding 'the health and safety of the client.' Usually it was wasting money on things like vegetables and organic protein cubes. I would have gotten upset, but I realized something. "So, if I don't die I'm going to make some cush? Silky."

"I'd have thought not dying would be 'silky' enough to motivate you to stay this side of the pavement."

"If I die, I don't have anything to worry about," I said. "If I survive, I'm still broke."

"Your reasoning defies logic," it said.

"While I'm out, why don't you make yourself useful and see what you can find out about Lou Lemon's old place and why she might be sore with Candy Cimarro."

"Way ahead of you, as usual," it said. "I'll send whatever I find to the office. Now get out of here. I'm working."

I flipped up my collar, stalked into the hallway, and slammed the door behind me. Working. More like surfing the feedreels and taking a nap.

I grumbled to myself the entire hack ride downtown. Early morning light broke through the dull overcast sky. I'd been up all night. At least it wasn't raining. I hoped Dickie had gotten word from Lou. No news was bad news at this point in the game.

But when I got to the office, I saw that bad news had gotten there before me.

Chapter Eight

I PUSHED OPEN THE etched glass door to see Dickie Roh leaning back in the chair behind my desk with his feet up on the filing cabinet and his mouth hanging open in a sonorous snore. Fiver Valiant, his burgundy braid smoothed and tightly rewoven down the centre of his shaved skull, flinched at the sound of the opening door and stared over his shoulder at me like a wounded rabbit.

He wore a simple, slim cut black suit jacket over a plain white t-shirt and a pair of grey jeans that looked a few sized too big for him. His face was bare of makeup. His blue eyes looked washed out, the whites were yellow, and he had dark circles dragging them down.

In his lap, he held the plain black briefcase I'd seen Candy Cimarro's goon load up his credit chips into. He gripped the edges with white knuckled fingers. He wore polished combat boots that looked like they saw more dance floors than street brawls, and he bounced his heels so fast that I thought he was going to wear a hole in my floor.

When it saw it was me, he relaxed. But only a little bit.

I closed the door behind me and hung up my coat and hat. Then I walked up behind Dickie and placed two fingers on the back of the chair behind his shoulders and pulled down slowly. When he was at a forty-five degree angle to the floor, his body sensed something was off and he gave a hypnic jerk that sent his feet flying. The chair shot out from underneath him and he landed on his back on the floor, staring up at me with wide eyes.

"Good morning, Dickie," I said. "Did you hear from Lou?"

"No-o-o," he said, as if trying to remember if it was true. Then he rolled onto his knees and stretched his back with a groan. "I might have fallen asleep, though."

"Why don't you go grab us some coffee," I said, and I held out my flesh hand to help him up off the floor. He nodded and rubbed the sleep from his eyes with his knuckles.

Then he turned toward the door and shrieked. Dickie grabbed me by both arms and swung me around, peeking over my shoulder like I was a shield.

"Bubs," he whispered. "We have a customer."

"I have a customer, Dickie." I reached up to break his iron grip on my arms. "You have an errand."

Dickie snapped his jaw shut and nodded. "Right," he said. "Coffee."

"And doughnuts," I said. "If you want me to forget about this."

"Doughnuts," he said. "Got it."

He snagged his coat and his hat off the rack and hustled out the door. The widow rattled in its fitting when it slammed closed behind him. I picked the chair up off the floor, spun it around on its base a couple of times, and then sat in it with my flesh and metal fingers steepled in front of my face. I said, "To what do I owe the pleasure, Mr. Valiant?"

The young man—not a boy at all, I could see without the makeup—cleared his throat and said, "Lou said if I ever got caught in the rain, you were the one to see."

I glanced out the window at the thin yellow light streaming in through the blinds. "It's not raining, brother."

"It's raining hard where I'm sitting," he said. His sweating hands slipped on the case and it clattered off his lap and onto the floor. He bent at the waist to pick it up, and then stopped. He sucked in a sharp breath and leaned forward carefully, trembling all over. When he had it in hand he dropped it on the desk in front of me and leaned back in his chair with a sigh. His pale skin had gone a shade of grey I usually only saw on corpses and I wondered what kind of glow up he was crashing down from.

"Lou Lemon and I go back a long ways," I said. I stared at the briefcase and wondered what two million credits felt like. "There's not much I wouldn't do for her. Playing backup for her last night, for example. That doesn't mean I'm interested in the same kind of games she is."

Valiant reached inside his jacket and pulled out a thin cigarette. He attempted to light it, but his fingers were shaking so badly he couldn't get the pocket burner to spark. I reached over the desk and took it from his clammy hands. When I held the flame for him he hesitated, then he leaned forward like he didn't want to get too close to me, and inhaled deeply. The smoke from the cigarette smelled faintly of vanilla. He blew twin streams out through his nose and slouched his shoulders.

"Lou is dead," he said. His voice was like his complexion, thin and pale and suddenly older.

My metal hand thumped onto the table between us and I let out the breath I'd been holding onto ever since my visit to the Spire. The chair creaked beneath me as I leaned back and spun towards the window. Shafts of golden light piercing through the murky dimness of my office.

He went on without prompting: "A couple of Cimarro's hard boys showed up at my apartment. I should have known she wouldn't let us get away with that money. We used to work together back—" He stopped himself. Tried again. "They got her with a small gun that looked like the one I keep under my mattress. It was gone when I looked for it afterward. I spent the night there with her dead on my carpet." He shuddered. "I had to."

I turned my chair so I could observe him from the corner of my eye. The young man crumpled in on himself, his shoulders shaking. His colourless eyes sank into the bruised flesh around them until only his stark white cheekbones seemed to have any shape to them. His nostrils were pink and raw on the outside as if he'd been snorting something. Maybe crying.

He shook his head and withdrew somewhere I couldn't touch him, but he whispered to himself as if he was in a dream: "They filled the case with the credit chips from the table and then gave me a certified untraceable transfer on holofilm that we were going to deposit on the way home. But Lou figured that's what they were waiting for, that they'd have our bank drops scoped out and we'd have goons on us the second we tried to make the deposit. Even with you tailing us, it wouldn't have been hard to do."

"Miss Candy lost the money in front of everybody there," I said. "It might have stung a little, but it was good press for Cat's Cradle."

Valiant's voice shook and he continued as if I hadn't spoken. "When we were leaving the club, we spotted one of those rental hacks with the fake chauffeurs. That's when Lou tried to get smart. She offered the driver a grand to trade vehicles, to bring her boiler to the hotel after a while. The driver had credits floating in her eyes at that. We made the switch. We felt bad about shaking you off, but Lou figured you wouldn't mind, and it might keep Cimarro's goons off of us if they were tailing you."

I said, "I met a couple of hard boys in Cimarro's parking lot. They didn't think too much of me."

Again, Valiant plowed ahead with his story, like it was eating him up inside and he had to get the words out before they killed him. He said, "Lou didn't want to go to the hotel either. So we took another cab over to my place. I live near the Red Zone—you know the kind of place, pay by the day, don't have to answer too many questions at the desk. We went upstairs and turned on the lights, and before we'd even kicked our shoes off this couple of thugs with those digifilm masks on come around the corner from the kitchen, their faces changing every couple of seconds. One was a tall lanky guy and the other one was short and soft around the middle with a chin that wobbled underneath the mask. Lou made a move to step in front of me and the guy must have thought she was going for a gun. The skinny guy shot her, just once, in the chest. It made such a dull crack—not loud at all—and I didn't know what had happened at first. Then Lou fell on the floor and she didn't move."

"Take a breath," I said. "We've got the time, don't we?"

Valiant lifted his hands to his face and rubbed furiously, like he was trying to bring back feeling to a numbed limb. When he dropped his hands, his eyes were bleary inside but sharper around the edges. He said, "Holy Origin I could use a drink."

As if on cue, Dickie crashed through the door carrying a box of doughnuts in one hand and a tray of disposable coffee cups in the other. The rich, astringent aroma of burnt beans wafted into the office like mana from the heavens. I stood and met him at the door, taking the food and drink so he could get his coat off. I brought the tray back to the desk and said, "Maybe not as strong as you'd like, but it should help."

I took the cup with the 'B' scrawled on top, knowing it would have double the cream and sugar a normal person would order. I sipped the syrupy liquid and sighed. Then I flipped open the box of doughnuts.

"Kreme Kween," I said to Dickie, lifting a pink-iced confection from the box. "You might be forgiven."

Dickie snagged a doughnut and eyed the shaken man across from me. He said, "You want me to wait outside?"

"Thanks, Dick," I said.

Dickie took his breakfast on the go and slipped out into the hallway. I figured he'd head downstairs to visit the buxom shop girl at LaundreLuxe to have a riveting conversation about the enzyme cleansers he seemed to have no end of interest in these days. When he closed the door, Valiant blinked and stared at the coffee in his hands as if he'd forgotten how it got there.

I lifted my cup toward him and said, "To Lou."

He nodded and sipped his drink. Then he shook his head and began talking again, like someone had hit pause on the feedreel in his head and decided to start it up again. He said, "These goons, they went over us. Searched my whole place. But we didn't have the credits on us. I'd gotten cold feet and asked Lou if we could stop at one of those all-night delivery places. I bought an expedited parcel delivery box and brought it out to the hack, and we packaged up the case and asked them to deliver it to my place in the morning. I paid three times as much as I should have to get a guaranteed delivery time of five o'clock. I think when they saw the address they got nervous, because its Red Line gang territory. They didn't dare say no. So

Cimarro's boys searched and searched but they couldn't find anything and Lou was dead and the short one held me down while the skinny one laid into me and I—" This time he had to stop and take a breath, his thin chest rose and fell rapidly like a bird stunned after hitting a window. "When I came to, they were gone. I was alone. Lou was dead."

"That was some quick thinking on your part." I pressed my lips together and licked the sugar off. "They'd have had to know you were going home. How'd they know where you live?"

"Candy and I used to—" His voice cracked. "I worked for her a long time ago. We never got along. But she'd know where to find me. We just didn't think of it. Probably she sent somebody to Lou's place, and the hotel too."

I rolled the compostable coffee cup between my hands and watched him carefully. "Tell me the rest."

"The delivery came right on time," he said. "As soon as I had the case, I came here."

I stood and took my coffee over to the window, peering out into the street. In daylight, the buildings looked greyer, the streets dirtier, the lights dingier. But at least it wasn't raining. I said. "Did they plant the gun?"

"Not that I saw," Valiant said. His voice had firmed up a little at the centre, if it was still frayed around the edges. "Not unless it was underneath her. I didn't check."

"If Cimarro has it in for you, something doesn't add up." I eyed a sausage cart that didn't normally frequent our block. The vendor seemed to sense me watching and looked up at the window. He didn't look away too quickly, so I let my gaze slide along the rest of the street. I continued, "You got off too easy. Did you and Lou talk much? She open up to you?"

When Valiant didn't answer I looked over my shoulder. He blushed and shook his head. "We had a more... physical relationship."

"Well," I sighed. "I'm sorry about Lou. But what did you think I was going to do about it?"

Valiant bit a pale lip and looked up at me with eyes that seemed to stare out from beyond the grave. He said, "Can't you help me?"

"I don't deal in revenge, if that's what you're after."

He pushed the shiny black case across the desk at me. He said, "Half of this money is mine. I won it fair and square."

"You won it by exploiting a flawed wheel," I said.

"I just called what Lou told me to call," he said. "That was our deal. Half of what's in this case is mine, and I'm not going to let Cimarro take me to the cleaners. But Lou's not here to spend her half. I'm not looking for revenge. I want a clean getaway. I want out of this town, baby. If I'd have called the law last night, they'd have found a way to weasel this cush into HCPD pockets. Don't tell me they wouldn't. But I... I think Lou would like you to have her half."

I whistled a low note and sank into my chair. The skin on the palm of my flesh hand itched and I rubbed it against the side of my leg. A million credits. "That's big money to flash around at a private dick, Valiant."

A smile quirked at the corner of his mouth and he glanced at me from beneath his bare eyelashes. "Don't I know it?"

"I think I'd better go have a look at your place," I said, tapping my metal fingers on the top of the case. "See what's broken."

He leaned forward suddenly and seemed to regret it. He sucked in quickly, and said, "Will you take care of the cush, Marlowe? We need to lay low, and I don't know what to do with it."

"Sure," I said. "I'll put it in the safe deposit drop downstairs. We'll each get a passcode. We'll talk split later on. But I've got a couple of favours to ask of you."

He bit his lip again and nodded warily.

"I need Candy Cimarro to know she needs to meet up with me," I said. "And I need you to take up temporary residence at a little rental I have a friend at. You'll be safer that way."

He nodded. I took the case downstairs and dropped it in the building's high security lockup and got two codes made: Valiant's was an alphanumerical job printed on a piece of ticker tape from at least three centuries ago; mine was a voice command. I scratched down his code onto a piece of paper for myself. We'd need both to get the safe open again, and I wasn't taking any chances.

When I got back upstairs, Fiver Valiant sat as still as a statue in the guest chair, staring at the place on the desk where the case had been. But he said he'd pinged Cat's Cradle and left a message for Miss Candy that he thought she'd understand.

Then we went downstairs and dragged Dickie away from the laundress. He drove us over to one of the rental units his parents used from time to time when they had out of town talent for their 'niche reels' visiting. I didn't ask what kind of niches they they catered to. A man named Jim Dolan gave us a room and said he'd be happy to ensure 'Mr. Black' wasn't bothered.

We got back in Dickie's car and he scanned the newsreels for any talk about Lou Lemon's death, but we found nothing. My shoulder ached where the upgrade was rubbing the wrong way. I scrubbed at my eyes and leaned against the window, hoping to catch a few winks before we got to Valiant's place in the Red Zone.

Chapter Nine

FIVER VALIANT'S ADDRESS TOOK us to a sagging square apartment building right next to the walls of metal scaffolding that surrounded the Red Zone, a gang controlled neighbourhood run by a sinister man who went by the name Mr. Vermillion. He didn't bother much with the world outside the Red Zone, but inside he ruled with a spiked iron fist. I didn't have much interest in going inside the zone, but I did want to avoid being seen by any of his henchmen. I had a feeling they might be better friends of Heavy John Harding than they were of mine.

I had Dickie drop me off on a side street, and I snuck over to where Valiant's building pressed up against twisted hedge of metal and electrical wires that marked the border of Vermillion's territory. Valiant's apartment was on the third floor, the middle window facing the Red Zone. He'd told me about the loose window he suspected the thugs had snuck in through and I figured I could use the same trick to avoid being seen by the front desk clerk.

They were bound to be reporting the comings and goings of their patrons to Mr. V.

As I climbed the rickety fire-escape stairs I cursed my ability to dig up trouble when I didn't have any business digging at all. At the top, I shimmied my fingers under the edge of the window and pushed the pane up with ease. Nice security, especially in the Grit. Most of the other windows on the building were equipped with the standard prison-bar accessory package that I would have expected. The edges of the window frame looked like it hadn't been that long since they'd been downgraded. I grabbed the top of the frame and swung my legs into the bedroom. There was nothing there that didn't belong. Nothing in the bathroom or the tiny kitchen and dining room. There was a lot of junk piled in the corners of the living room, fancy clothes with the price scanners still attached and a black market demagnetizer used for taking out the little alarm signals and tracking devices highbinder thread shops were so fond of using. Fiver Valiant had a nice little boutique of stolen runway fashions, but other than that there was nothing of interest in the apartment.

There was no body on the floor. No blood, either.

A chill crept up my spine and tickled the back of my neck. There were footsteps walking too slowly in the corridor. I cursed and sprinted for the bedroom. I scrambled out of the window and swung myself over the railing of the fire escape. I dropped to the next landing, then did it once more and dropped to the ground. There was a sound from the windows above me, but I didn't look back. I didn't want the last thing I saw to be the barrel of a gun.

I ran as fast as I could back to Dickie's car, jumped in, and said, "Get us out of here."

Dickie's eyes went wide. He used the manual function to punch the boiler into high gear and hit the grid going twice the legal limit. I squeezed my eyes shut as the auto controls took over and the car lurched into the stream of traffic. When we didn't die, Dickie said, "Did you find Lou?"

"I don't think Lou was ever in that apartment," I said and I swore under my breath. I rubbed my flesh hand over my face and laughed. "That wasn't my finest moment, Dickie, I gotta admit."

Dickie laughed too, a little nervously. "What happened?"

"I knew the kid's story didn't quite add up," I said. "Do me a favour and ring up your parent's building. Have Dolan give Mr. Black a service call."

Dickie keyed the number into his tattler and did as I said. I listened with a grim smile on my face as Dolan apologized and explained that Mr. Black must have just stepped out for some fresh air. When Dickie killed the call, I muttered, "I don't think there's much fresh about Valiant's story. It's starting to stink something fierce."

Dickie crossed his pudgy arms over his chest. The slick, pin-striped number he was wearing probably cost more than I'd made all of last year, including the time I worked for the HCPD. His usually cheerful face sagged a little, his round cheeks hanging like jowls over the tight, starched collar of his shirt.

"What?" I said. "Nobody tried to shoot at you."

"We're getting you a new tattler," he said.

"I'm gonna see if Rae has a used one I can rent for a while," I said. "Next time she refits my arm. Don't worry about it."

The farther we got from the Red Zone the more my shoulders began to relax. I'd been sure I was dead meat for a minute there. Mittens would have been pissed.

"I am worried about it," he said. "If you get in trouble like this, you can't call for help. Not me or Rae, not even the HCPD. At least let me get you a handheld one you can keep in your pocket."

I gritted my teeth. I couldn't even afford to pay Dickie for the secretarial work he did for me. He just hung around with me because he liked it. I gave him a hard time about not being a "real" detective, not because I didn't think he could do the work, but because I refused to have him put his life on the line for nothing. I knew he didn't mean to do it, but the way Dickie flashed his cush around really set my teeth on edge. A handheld tattler was chump change to someone with his bankroll. He didn't think anything of offering to buy me one. My face burned thinking of how long I'd have to scrimp and save before I could even get my hands on a used one.

But he was right.

I clenched my metal hand into a fist and pounded the top of my thigh with it while I stared out the window, hating myself for all the crappy choices that had led me to this pathetic place. Then I thought of the case full of credit chips in my safe deposit box and I smiled grimly.

"Let's go to the hockmarket then," I said after a while. "And I'm going to pay you back."

Dickie sighed and sagged with relief. His cheeks squished into his eyes with his trademark smile and he knocked his hat back to wipe his forehead with the pink handkerchief he'd pulled from his pocket. I'd gotten it for his last birthday. Rae had helped me pick it out and haggled the shop keep down on the price because she was buying three new Cosmo Régale handbags and he couldn't say no. I tried to stay grumpy but I couldn't help but smile back at him.

He keyed the coordinates in the control console and rubbed his hands together. "I know just the place."

While we drove, I told him about what had happened in the apartment and I tossed around a couple of my theories about Lou Lemon and the licorice Prince. He listened intently with a fist propped under his chin and his eyes as wide as if he were watching some never-seen-before classic cinema footage of one of his favourite noir actresses.

When I finished, the boiler was rolling up to a bustling market square in the centre of the Grit District. Dickie connected to the office holophone to check for updates from Mittens.

A single, terse message said, "These guys are good. The data is scrambled. All I've got is that it was Lou Lemon's licence that went to Candy Cimarro and the Cat's Cradle—"

"Thanks for nothing, pussycat," I muttered. "I already had that much."

Mittens' message continued after a pause and I pictured the irritating little cat licking it's nanoparticled bung hole. "—Oh, and HoloCity General has a Jane Doe matching Lemon's description. The body was stripped of identifying tech and dropped a few blocks from the Spire. HCPD hasn't bothered to run the biologics in her yet, but I'd be willing to bet it's your client. That's all. Try not to die."

The message ended with a click. I punched my metal fist a little too hard into the palm of my flesh hand and cursed. "Damn that cat. I could have used that intel before I climbed into Valiant's trap."

"On that happy note... " Dickie clapped his hands together. "Time for some retail therapy."

"You sound like Rae," I said, scowling at him.

"Look on the bright side," he said. "You're not dead. And we get to go shopping."

"Shopping is a lot more fun if you actually have a load of cush to blow."

Dickie parked the boiler and slid out onto the street. He held his hand out to me in gentlemanly fashion. "Today, you get to blow my load."

I snorted.

"Holy Origin, Bubs." His eyes went wide and he dropped his hand. "That's not what I meant. I mean, not that I wouldn't, but you know... You're like my—" He fumbled for a suitably sterile term. "—colleague."

"I can't believe you used to work in the PornoPop industry," I said, shaking my head. I pushed him out of the way and climbed out of the car myself. "And for the record, I'm your boss."

"I'm more like a volunteer than an employee."

"Yes," I said. I grabbed him by the hand and pulled him toward the hockmarket. "And you've volunteered to do my bidding."

He pulled his collar up to hide his blushing cheeks. "It sounds kind of dirty when you put it like that."

The hockmarket bustled with vendors pulling two wheeled carts stacked precariously high, shoppers carrying bags and boxes, and hustlers jumping between them like fleas on a stray dog. Colourful awnings and flashing lights competed to draw the eye of customers. Tables at more permanent shop fronts were laden with everything from computer chips and cybernetic upgrades to black market meat and imitation fashions.

"Come on," I said. "Let's get this over with."

Dickie winked at me over the collar of his coat. "I bet you say that to all the boys."

He darted off into the crowd before I could hit him.

Chapter Ten

I TRIED TO FOLLOW the top of Dickie's head as he wound his way through the vendor stalls in the main part of the square. Then he ducked into a narrow alley tucked between two buildings. A tiny red sign above the opening blinked with the words TOM TOM'S COMM-COMMS.

I rolled my eyes and followed him into the dank corridor. The buildings on either side were so tall they blocked out all the natural light, but a couple of strings of tiny orange lights ran in an arrow pattern pointing toward a door at the back of the alley. It stank like all the kinds of things the Grit usually stank of and I wished I had a flashlight to check where I was stepping. I only had so many clothes to ruin. I squinted my eyes in the thin light filtering in from the street. A shadow fell over the mouth of the alley behind me, and the alley dropped into darkness. The orange lights flickered. But when I turned to look over my shoulder, there was no one there.

The back of my neck prickled as I crept farther into the alley.

"Hey, Dickie," I called out. "Wait for me."

He didn't reappear. I said a few words that would have gotten my mouth washed out with soap if my mother was still around. Dickie must have gone in through the door. I couldn't see any other way to get out of the alley. I picked my way carefully through the dark. I wrinkled my nose and hoped wouldn't step in anything squishy. As my eyes adjusted, I thought I could see the shape of bags of garbage piled along the side of the right wall. I hugged the wall to my left, in case the garbage piles had people sleeping in them. A shadow blocked my light again and once again, I couldn't see anything in front of me.

I whirled to face the mouth of the alley. A huge man stood, his shoulders nearly touching the buildings on each side. I backed up and tripped on something behind me, landing flat on my butt in the greasy puddles I had been trying not to step in. The man approached with a fat rectangular shape in his fat rectangular fist.

"Bubbles Marlowe," he said. "You're comin' with me."

"I don't think so." I scrambled backward into the pile of trash, suddenly hoping there was someone sleeping in there, someone I could toss at this goon before I ran for my life. A box broke beneath my weight and I got my metal arm wedged between two thin shards of bent metal.

"I don't recall asking," the man said. The rectangle in his hand sparked and flickered.

I kicked out at the man as he got closer, praying now that Dickie wouldn't come and look for me, that he'd stay and have a nice long conversation with Tom Tom and his Comm-Comms. The big man grabbed my flailing leg in one huge fist and lunged at me with the other.

The blue arc of electricity on his taser was the last thing I saw before my body exploded with pain and I forgot all about Dickie and Tom Tom and the dirty back alley. My last thought before I passed out from the shock was that I was sorry Mittens was going to lose all those credits on me.

###

I came awake with a jolt and a gold toothed goon grinning down at me with a halo of light behind his head.

I winced and said, "God?"

The man laughed like a barrel full of rusted metal scraps being stirred by a stick of dynamite. A syringe glinted in his hand and I brought my flesh fingers up to my throat where it felt like I'd gotten bitten by a diseased rat.

"What the hell did you stick me with?" I groaned. "Tetanus and Plague?"

"Just a little jolt for the adrenals." He giggled some more, like adrenal stims weren't one of the most addictive drugs on the black market. "The boss wants you wide awake for you meeting."

His grinding laughter was starting to grind on my nerves. My flesh prickled all over like there were spiders dancing the tarantella over my body. I said, "Candy Cimarro?"

"Miss Candy?" He giggled again. "I said, the boss. The big boy."

In my mind I watched my metal hand tear into his throat and pull his voice box out like a piece of stale bubble gum and crush it between my fingers. Instead, my upgrade spasmed and twisted the skin underneath painfully. The taser must have fried something inside it. So I said, "All right, I'll play. Who's the big boy?"

He grabbed me by the back of the coat and lifted me up off the floor. My legs felt a little weak underneath me and my brain was trying to ooze out my ears, but I managed to stay upright. He said, "I guess you'll find out, soon enough."

I didn't have an answer to that, so I stepped where he wanted me to step, and we made our way slowly down a long, grey corridor. It seemed like the kind of underground bunker a guy might use if he was scared of nuclear bombs or raiding Vikings.

As my wits slowly came back to me I wondered why, if Lou had been killed outside the Spire, the killers didn't get the money. And if she really had been killed in Valiant's apartment, why somebody had taken the trouble to carry her all the way back to the Biz District.

I didn't have long enough to sort it out before the thug steered me around a corner and into a closed door. It wasn't so bad, if you didn't mind having a flat face. He let his hand drop from the back of my neck and knocked on the door with a dandified rat-a-tat-tat.

"Get out of the way," he said and pulled me back like I was standing so close just to make his life difficult.

The stim he'd poked me with was waking up inside my veins, making all my senses come alive. Painfully, that meant his grating voice and onion-smelling armpits were dialed up to eleven and the thinking part of my brain was walking around in circles looking for a way out of my skull.

"Come in," a deep, nasal voice said over a hidden intercom.

The door broke in the middle and swung inward. The meat brick behind me shoved me on the shoulder and I stumbled into the room, trying to get my half-numbed legs to point in the same direction. After a few awkward dance moves I managed to find my way to a chair and collapsed into it gratefully.

"Bubbles Marlowe," the nasal voice said. "Please sit down."

The voice was coming from behind an outrageously high-backed black chair sitting opposite a desk that seemed to be made of highly polished concrete. In fact, all of the walls and the floor were made out of the same material. On opposite sides of the throne-like chair hung two flags. One I recognized from my days as a beat cop as the emblem of the Eastern Sprawl's largest weapon smugglers. The other was pure red, as if it had been dipped in fresh blood. Large men stood next to the flags like bookends to the ridiculous tableau. I glanced over my shoulder to see that my gold-toothed kidnapper seemed to have cloned himself. He and his twin stood on opposite sides of the door. One of them grinned at me and made a "turn around" motion with his fingers. He mouthed the words, "Big Boy."

I turned around.

The high-backed chair turned around.

The round, grim face of Heavy John Harding was on the other side. He smiled at me, just the way he had seemed to in the courthouse vidfeed. The effect was somewhat dampened by the fluffy white puppy he held on his lap, with a little yellow bow in a fountain on top of its head. The dog wagged its tail. I tried not to stare at it.

"How nice of you to join me here, Ms. Marlowe," Harding said. "I've so been looking forward to meeting you."

I peeled my tongue off the top of my mouth and said, "Thanks for the invite. Maybe next time you could try sending a text message instead."

The fat rolls on Harding's forehead clumped together like the skin that formed on the top of stagnant sewer water. "Did Beasley not treat you like a lady?"

"He shocked me with a taser and then shot me full of drugs," I said. "I'm sure treating me like a lady is exactly what he thought he was doing."

"I'm a busy man, Marlowe," he said. "You'll have to forgive my methods. I don't have time to dicker, even with a celebrity such as yourself."

"What do you want with me, Harding?"

He smiled at me with perfect teeth, except that they were far too small for his face. He said, "You're the one who fingered Sammy West. It won't do."

I wiggled my fingers and toes a little, hoping the effects of the stim and the taser were wearing off. My head still ached, but my brain seemed to come back to me slowly.

"Politics are a complicated thing," Harding went on in his droning nasal voice. "I wouldn't expect someone like you to understand. It can be very hard on the nerves. You know me, don't you Marlowe? You've heard enough, I'm sure. I'm a hard man. I'm hard and I'm flush and there's not much I want in the world anymore. But the things I want, they dig their claws into me and they won't let go until I have them. Do you know what I mean?"

"Sounds like you're sampling too much of your wares," I said. I stared at the fluffy dog on his lap, trying to decide if it was a real animal or a high-end nanoskin.

"She's a funny one," Harding said over his shoulder to one of the statue-like guards. "She's a comedian."

The dog yipped and wagged its tail at me. I wrinkled my nose at it and stuck out my tongue.

Harding spun back around and I pulled my tongue back into my mouth. The smile fell off his face. "You're not going to be laughing for long, Marlowe."

I flexed my metal fingers against the side of my leg. The upgrade seemed to be coming back to life, at least. Harding watched me with eyes, like his teeth, that seemed undersized above the massive cheeks and jowls. He seemed like he was waiting for me to say something. I cleared my throat. "Is that so?"

"When I do want something, I'm not all that particular about how I get it. I don't have to be. You catch my drift?"

The dog blinked at me. I tried not to break eye contact with Harding, but the fluffy little face was impossible not to look at. I grinned in spite of myself.

"Sure," I said. "And with all that power and cush and these hard boys in your pocket, you woke up one day and said to yourself, 'You know what's missing in my life? You know what would really make me happy? It's not the power games and politics and pro skirts and blow... What I need is a poodle with a cute little yellow bow on its head—'"

A grating giggle burst out behind me. Heavy John Harding glowered at Beasley and placed his big hands on top of the polished concrete table. He lifted the index finger on his right hand, and the big guy behind him on the right side pulled out a charged plasma rifle and let off a single blue bolt. It hissed through the air past my left ear and there was a heavy thud. The giggling stopped. The little dog jumped off of Harding's lap and strode to the edge of the desk and sat there, still staring at me.

Harding looked at me as if nothing had happened and I resisted the urge to look at the body I knew was laying behind me. He said, very softly, with a faint smile on his wide lips, "You killed Lou Lemon."

"That's an interesting theory," I said with careful neutrality. The hairs on my scalp lifted and a chill ran down my spine as I began to see the missing pieces in the puzzle.

Harding went on. His eyes glittered and his jowls quivered, but otherwise he held onto his excitement. He said, "You killed Lou Lemon. Maybe she needed to be bumped off, I have no opinion on that. But it was you who pulled the trigger. She was shot once, through the heart with an old-school twenty-two. There's x-ray camera footage from Candy Cimarro's place showing you packing a twenty-two last night, and your employee file from the HCPD has you listed as a pretty sharp shooter. When you were at the Cradle, you watched Lemon win a bunch of money. You were supposed to be her bodyguard, but you got a better idea. You followed her and the boy toy over to the Spire, gave her a piece of your mind, and made off with the cush."

The little dog leaped off the desk and landed in my lap. I scratched it behind the ears with my flesh hand. It was warm and furry, felt just like the real deal. It wagged its tail and licked my fingers.

"You made a deal with the boy," Harding said, "but it didn't stick and he cut town. That don't matter though. Because Chief Swain has your gun along with Lemon's body. And you've got the cush."

I straightened the bow on the dog's head and said, "Is there a tag out for me?"

"Not until I say so. . . Swain won't know its your gun or that it's Lemon's body until I give the word. . . I got a lot of friends, you know."

I took a deep breath and let it out slowly through my nose, considering my options. I said, "I got knocked on the head outside of the Cradle. My own fault for getting distracted. When I woke up, my gun was gone. I never caught up with Lou, never saw her again. The boy came to me this morning with the cush in a briefcase and a story that Lou had been killed back at his place. That's how I have the cush—for safekeeping. I knew the boy's story didn't line up, but his handing over the money made me want to believe him. Lou was a friend of mine, so I had to look into it."

"You should have let the cops do that," Harding said, barely containing his tiny-toothed grin.

"I thought there was a chance the boy was being framed," I said. "And, of course, there was a chance I might be able to make rent this month. Legitimately. It has been done once or twice, even in HoloCity."

The dog yipped again and wagged its tail. Harding leaned over the desk and reached a fat finger into the dog's face. It licked him once and batted at the finger with a paw, then curled up in my lap and tucked its nose under its tail. Harding crossed his arms on the desk and said, "Two mil, and the boy toy just passed it over to you to keep. There ain't a jury in the city who would buy that line from you, Marlowe. You got the cush. Lou was killed with your gun. The boyfriend is gone, but I could bring him back if I wanted to. He might make a good witness if we needed one. You know how the feedreels love a good witness."

I stroked the dog's fur and stared at Harding's guards. They each had a plasma rifle tucked into their sides, and I could see the holster of a pistol or a taser weapon inside the jacket of the one who'd shot my giggling kidnapper. His jacket had folded over when he'd replaced his rifle. I guessed the other guards had a similar arsenal. I had to keep

Harding talking if I was going to have any chance to get out of there alive.

"Was the play at Cat's Cradle rigged?"

"Of course," Harding said. He reached into his pocket and pulled out a clear glass pipe full of tiny grains of crystal. He lit the pipe and drew in a lungful of noxious yellow smoke which oozed out his nostrils like he'd sprung a leak. He said, "The croupier, a skid named Ainslo, was in on it. Copper button on the floor, on the croupier's shoe, wires up the leg. Same old crap that's been fleecing punters for centuries."

"Miss Candy didn't act like she knew anything was crooked."

Harding clapped his hands together and said, "She knew it was wired. She didn't know her head croupier had a score to settle."

"Ainslo can't be sleeping too good," I said. "She's not the kind of woman I'd like to cross."

"Haven't you?" Harding said. He frowned and waved his pipe at me, making my eyes burn. "Ainslo's taken care of anyway. And it wasn't a flashy play. They didn't win all the time. They couldn't. The old tricks aren't perfect."

"You seem to know a lot about it."

I leaned back in my chair and rolled my shoulders. The upgrade still pinched, but the pain and fogginess in my head had been pushed aside by adrenaline. My luckless abductor must have kept a little of my stim dose for himself, because it hadn't lasted as long they'd intended. But I didn't want to let that on. I closed my eyes halfway and tried to look relaxed.

"I'm impressed," I said. "And flattered. Was all of this just to set me up for the big squeeze?"

Harding flashed the little white teeth at me again and his eyes disappeared into gleeful folds of flesh. "You'd like that, wouldn't you? But no. Some of it was planned, some just happened, the way the best plans always do. Don't be sore about it Marlowe, it ain't personal. I've got connections I gotta keep happy, you know how it is."

"Right," I said. "Like Sammy West."

"Sammy West can rot in that cell," Harding said, scowling like an overfed house pet that didn't get his extra helping of sausage. "He should never have gotten caught. He was supposed to take care of that camera before he took care of the broad, but he got cocky. Thought his buddy Swain would help him get rid of the vidfeed. His bad luck that there were two witnesses, too. And one of them was you."

"I'd have thought Swain would jump at the chance to take another swing at me," I said.

"Swain can't go after you publicly," Harding said. "He tried once and failed, now he's got to have someone else do it. His connections in the Grit don't like to see him picking on one of their own. You've got more friends than you realize, Marlowe. And if anyone bumps you off now, it's going to look even worse for me."

"So what do you want me to do about it?" I said. "Commit suicide?"

Harding laughed and relit his pipe. His eyes went slightly unfocussed as he inhaled, but they landed on me like a pair of lead weights. "Witnesses make mistakes," he said. "Even slick private dicks like yourself. I was thinking you might like to rethink your statement. Have a change of heart and put it in writing."

"Then I'd be under a perjury rap." I curled my lip at him and leaned forward in my chair, the dog whimpered and scrambled to stay on my lap. "Which I couldn't beat. I'd rather try my hand at the murder rap."

"You'd just have to try to beat it," Harding said. "The feedreels are playing this as me against you. If you're on shaky ground, I can drum up enough press to get back in the good graces of the board. If not, I've gotta fight with my teeth."

"And what about the two mil?" I played with the little yellow bow on the dog's head and felt its warm tongue on my wrist.

"If you want to play, it could be yours," Harding said. "It ain't my cush after all. If West gets cleared, I might be tempted to add a little icing to the cake."

I nodded and scratched the dog behind the ear. I was getting bored of this conversation. Harding's henchmen looked bored. The flags hung limply behind the concrete desk and they looked bored.

"Catch," I said.

Harding blinked. "What?"

I grabbed the dog by the scruff of the neck and tossed it into the air above Harding's head. He lunged to his feet with his eyes wide. The guards looked confused as to whether they should try to shoot me or catch the dog. I planted my metal hand on the desk and launched myself to the other side, slipped my hand inside the jacket of the first guard and pulled out his pistol.

Harding caught the dog. All three guards pointed their guns at me. I had my pistol pressed against the back of Harding's fat skull.

"The big boy gets it first, brothers," I said to the guards. Sweat beaded on Harding's forehead. The dog jumped off his lap and ran to the other side of the room, yelping with its tail between its legs. I whispered in the fat man's ear, "Now's the time you start praying that you've been a good boss, Harding. You trust your men to try to stop me? Or are you gonna let me walk out of here?"

"Take it easy," he grunted to his goons. To me he said, "This is pointless, Marlowe. Where are you going to go from here. If I wanted to have you knocked off I would have done it. You can't shoot anybody here without getting in a worse scrape than if you went with my plan."

I looked at each of the guards in turn. The one I'd taken the pistol from sneered at me and his friend had murder in his eyes. But the guard by the door still looked bored, as if this was just another day for him.

Harding shifted in his seat. "Well, Marlowe?"

"I'm leaving," I said. I pointed at the guard next to the door. "I'm taking him with me to operate the doors on the way out. I don't want to have to shoot anybody, but if that's how it's gotta be I'm not going to flinch. You let me go, and I'll forget about this conversation."

Harding shrugged lazily and his cheeks twitched with a smile. He said, "And then?"

"You get a better handle on your deal," I said. "If you throw enough protection behind me that I don't have to worry about Swain anymore, I'd be tempted to throw in with you. . . and if you're as hard as you say you are, a few hours won't hurt you while we figure it out."

"You know, Marlowe." Harding laughed and picked up his broken pipe off the desk. He dropped the pieces in a trash bin next to his feet. "I'm beginning to see why Swain doesn't like you."

"You're going to let me go?"

"It's an idea I can work with," he said. He opened the drawer of his desk and pulled out another pipe, just like the one I'd broken. Lit it, and let the smoke waft up toward me. My eyes burned and I held my breath as he sucked in another lungful of poison. His shoulders relaxed. "Seb, keep your rod to yourself and show the lady outside."

The guard by the door tucked his pistol back inside its holster and nodded. I sidled around the desk, keeping my sights trained on the substantial target of Heavy John Harding's round head. The goons behind him glowered at me. Seb opened the inside door and I stepped through. Harding smiled and waved. I didn't drop the gun until Seb came through and the door closed behind us. Then I got the hell out of there as fast as Heavy John's hard boy could lead me through the maze.

I had a long, thoughtful hack ride back to the office from the outer reaches of the Biz District.

Chapter Eleven

THERE WAS AN ARGUMENT coming from inside the office when I arrived. Dickie's frantic pacing and rising voice echoed down the hallway as I made my way through the building. Another voice, low and rumbling, seemed to ooze through the cracks. I listened at the door for a while, with my heart beating hard in my chest. I groaned as my ears confirmed my suspicions.

I closed my eyes and pressed my forehead against the frosted glass for a moment before opening the door. The voices stopped. I stepped through the doorway to find three drawn faces staring at me. Dickie had lost his hat and his slicked back hair was sticking up at odd angles. His pudgy cheeks sagged below exhausted eyes. Rae Adesina, my best friend and tech guru, stood by the window with her long arms crossed over her chest. Her dark skin glistened with expensive cosmetics that didn't even smudge with the tears pouring from her eyes. Both of them lit up when I came through the door. I gave them a small wave before glaring at the other person in the room.

"I hope you didn't come for my funeral, Tom," I said to the lantern-jawed, barrel-chested lump stuffed into an ill-fitting grey HCPD uniform. "You're a bit early."

Detective Tom Weiland, my ex-partner and ex-friend, turned an alarming shade of purple and bunched his massive hands into fists at his side. He took a step toward me like he wanted to clobber me. I met him with a defiant stare. He stopped in his tracks and turned his head away from me. I thought I saw a glimmer in the corners of his grey eyes.

"For gritssake, Marlowe," he said. He ran a thick hand through is black hair and blew out a breath of air through puffed cheeks. "We thought you were dead."

"Everyone keeps saying that," I said. "And yet here I am."

Dickie broke out of his stupor. He crossed the office in three bounding steps and barrelled into me with wide open arms. He picked me up and spun me around.

"I'm so glad you're okay, Bubbles," he said with his face plastered against my chest. "I came out of the comm shop to check on you, and I saw a big guy dragging your body out of they alley. I thought you were a goner."

Then his grip slipped and he dropped me clum-sily back to my feet.

"Oof—" he said. "You're really heavy."

I frowned at him and straightened my coat. "It's the arm."

"Speaking of which..." Rae said, wiping her eyes, and stomping towards me on a pair of electric blue pumps that looked like they could double as weapons in a back alley brawl. "You were due for a refit two weeks ago."

I flinched as she grabbed my shoulder and tore into the connective sensors with long, painted fingernails. I said, "Is that why it's starting to pinch?"

"You know, when someone gives you a cybernetic prosthetic worth hundreds of thousands of credits," she said. "It would be considered polite if you at least attempted to keep up with regular maintenance."

"Ouch," I said. "I'm sorry, okay? I am not good at that kind of thing. Schedules. Appointments." I narrowed my eyes at Tom. "I even managed to get my testimony time wrong, thanks to some meddling by Chief Swain."

"How many times do I have to tell you," he snarled at me. "Stay out of Swain's way. What do you think you're doing teaming up with D.A. Fairweather on a case like this? Do you want to die?"

"No, I don't," I said. "Much as I'm sure that annoys your boss. And I'm also not going to stop living my life in order to stay breathing. Deal with it."

Tom turned away in disgust.

Rae got the last of the connection undone. She twisted the upgrade off my stump and I felt the weight lift off of my shoulder with a wet, sucking sensation. Rae hissed under her breath.

"Holy Origin, Bubbles," she said. "Why didn't you come to see me? You've got open blisters under the sensors."

"I've been busy," I said, rolling the scarred remains of my natural arm around in circles. "Do you know how many pissant jobs I have to do every week just to afford this office space? Doesn't help that half my clients can't afford to pay."

"Dickie, grab my kit for me please," Rae said. She pushed her black-framed glasses up into her curly blue hair with one hand, holding the upgrade up with the other. Rae Adesina might look like a runway model playing a mad scientist, but she was a tough cookie. The sugar-free, organic kind that look like something you might like to eat but that will crack your teeth if you try to bite into them.

Dickie eagerly hopped to do her bidding, adoration in his eyes. She took the kit from him and passed him the arm. His eyes bulged and his arms sagged under the weight. "You weren't kidding," he said. "This thing's a beast."

Rae opened her tool kit and pulled out a jar of analgesic salve. I gritted my teeth as she wiped down my stump with an antiseptic wipe. The areas where I'd thought the limb was pinching burned like she was applying acid to them. As she rubbed the salve, the pain dulled and a cooling sensation replaced it. She said, "You really couldn't tell how bad this was?"

I shrugged. "I guess the scar tissue isn't as sensitive as the rest of my skin."

"You mean there's part of her that isn't calloused?" Tom muttered under his breath.

I whipped my head around. "Excuse me, Tom, would you like to say that so the class can hear?"

"Taking care of herself has never been Marlowe's strong suit." Tom refused to look at me.

"What's the matter, Tom?" I said. "Can't stand to face the consequences of your decisions?"

"What Swain did to you is not my fault." My former partner whirled on me. He clenched his fists at his sides a shouted, "I warned you to back off of that case and you wouldn't listen. Just like you won't listen now. What the hell do you think you're doing playing around with Biz District politics? Why don't you face the truth, Marlowe? You don't give a gritsucking damn for anyone but yourself. You've got a death wish, and the rest of us are just forced to stand by and watch you self-destruct."

Rae held her breath as she worked on my arm and I could see by the light flashing behind her dark eyes that she had a thing or two she'd like to say to Tom Weiland. It had been her boyfriend Jimi's murder that I was investigating when Swain decided I was a liability to his side hustle.

But Rae had known Tom and I long enough to know there was no sense in getting involved in one of our blow outs. She grabbed her tools and got to work on the upgrade, her jaw muscles clenched tight.

"For your information, Detective Weiland," I said, my voice cracking, "I was meeting with Mayor Randall to see about a charity grant when she was shot. Part of her upcoming campaign was to help start up businesses in the Grit. She'd chosen me as one of the potential candidates because of my service to the community. I foolishly thought it might be nice to get paid for some of the work I do. So, I guess you're right. Thinking about myself is what got me into this mess."

Tom had grace enough to look a little sheepish under his bluster. He turned away again and stalked over to the window with his hand stuffed in his pockets and his rounded shoulders hunched sulkily.

"So, uh, Bubs?" Dickie's eyes darted nervously between me and my former partner. He licked his lips. "What happened to you in the alley?"

I gave them the short version of my conversation with Heavy John Harding while Rae worked on my arm. I left out a few details, including the fact that I had over two million holocreds in my safe deposit box downstairs. Tom's posture revealed that he was listening carefully. I tried to burn a hole in his back with my eyes.

Rae brought the upgrade back over to me and pursed her lips like she was trying to decide what she wanted to say. She said, "You aren't done with this yet."

"I gotta do what I can for Lou," I said. "She deserves that much. But I can't do it without help. I'm going to bring in the brass."

Tom's head snapped up.

"You?" Rae's eyes nearly popped out of her head. "You are willingly going to the cops?"

Tom turned his shoulder slightly and watched me out of the corner of his eye.

"Not the cops," I said. "A cop."

"I'm not doing it, Marlowe," Tom said, his wide mouth pulled down into a frown. "I'm sorry you're in this mess but I can't afford to put my career on the line every time you—"

"I meant Bernie Howes," I said, and Tom's shoulders sank.

He said, "Howes? What do you wanna see that pencil pusher for?"

"You don't want to be involved in this and I respect that, Tom." I enjoyed the look of guilt tugging at the corners of his eyes. I said, "But if you could get a message to him, I'd be grateful."

Tom leaned against the wall next to the window and rubbed his hands over his face. He looked more tired every time I saw him. Part of me felt sorry for the guy—a career cop with aspirations of getting into politics, lamed up by his own moral integrity. Mostly, I just felt sad. Tom followed the letter of the law and I followed the spirit. Somehow the two paths never quite seemed to meet up.

"All right, Marlowe," he said. "I'll set it up."

"Thanks," I said.

He pushed himself off the wall and stomped across the room. I held out a hand to him as he passed, but he brushed it away.

"Don't," he said. He opened the door and stepped into the hall. My hand dropped back down to my side and an ache formed in my chest like a cold, hard knot.

Before he closed the door, he turned over his shoulder and said, "And don't ask me for any more favours after this, Marlowe. I'm glad you're not dead. But there's only so many times I can take a call like that. We're done, after this."

The door clicked closed with a sound like the cock of a hammer.

Chapter Twelve

I WAS TO MEET Bernie Howes, D.A. Fairweather's chief investigator, at a pop-up market about three blocks from HCPD headquarters. Detective Weiland had sent an encrypted message to my tattler, which Rae had fixed before she and Dickie left my office. The ping had come from a line I didn't recognize, but I figured he had a right to be cautious. Weiland knew the kind of man Chief Swain was, and he'd been under tight surveillance after my plasma rifle 'accident.' I couldn't really blame him for not wanting to get involved.

Rather, I shouldn't have. But I did.

A sour taste burned in the back of my mouth as I scanned the bustling market area, and I tried to forget about my once-friend. The little square was a hive of activity. Most of the vendors were shilling things like lab-grown produce, imitation meats, and flashy low-tech toys for kids. This was the kind of place you came to buy groceries after work, not hustle for black market organs.

I spotted a food cart I recognized and decided to grab something to eat. Dickie had snuck some credits into my coat pocket before he left and, as much as it had annoyed me to find them, it was hard to say no to HoloCity street food. I stepped up to the cart and was greeted by a pair of bright black eyes in a russet brown face and a flash of white teeth. The kid said, "Hey, Marlowe! What's the smoke? I hear you're on the run from some big bads these days. Silky, man. Just like an action reel hero."

"Ricky," I said, smiling back at him. "You're moving up in the world. No more dish scrubbing for you?"

"You know how it is," the boy said, the world-weary tone to his voice at odds with his young face. "Hard to keep good workers in the Grit. I only stay 'cause Mama needs the money and Mr. Santano lets me eat all the noodles I want. What can I get for you? I hardly recognized you with the hat and the collar. You really are in hiding, huh?"

I ordered myself a large noodle bowl and let him prattle on while he worked. When he was done, I ate my meal leaning against the cart and watching the other patrons of the market. Ricky chatted up each customer like a professional, upselling them on the special and earning a decent number of tips. It hurt to see such a bright kid with so much hustle grinding away for a few cred each day. He enjoyed it now, but how long until he realized the Grit was a dead end and no amount of hustling ever got a Grit skid out of the hole they were born in.

A tall man with thin arms and legs and a round potbelly approached the cart and ordered the same thing I had. He nodded to me as Ricky prepared the food, and said, "I guess it's getting pretty hot out here for you, eh, Marlowe?"

The overcast clouds above us had held onto all the moisture they could handle. A fine mist was suspended in the air, thickening into a cloud of white the farther up and out I looked. The cold and damp of it got under my skin. I was anything but hot. Still, I knew what he meant.

"You're Fairweather's man?" I asked, tossing the compostable bowl in the green trash bin reserved for organics.

He shook my hand with cool, dry fingers. A thick reddish moustache jumped as he smiled at me with crooked, yellow teeth.

"Bernie Howes," he said. "I've got a car waiting for us. Best not to talk too much in public."

When Ricky passed him his noodles, he motioned for me to follow him into the crowd. But the kid called me back and I stopped.

"Hey Marlowe," he said. "Wait a minute. I got a coupon for you."

I groaned and turned back to the food cart. The kid held a piece of transparent holofilm between his fingers that could be coded for a number of different discounts. He beckoned me with his fingers. The scent of salty bone broth, garlic, and green onions hung thick in the air as I leaned on the counter. I said, "Hurry up kid, I'm on a case."

"There's a big guy in a grey coat been watching you ever since you came up to my cart," Ricky said in a stage whisper, his eyes darting over my shoulder. Then he grinned widely and raised his voice so everyone could here, "You come back and see us again real soon, ma'am!"

I spun around in time to see the tail of a trench coat disappear behind an awning hung with cheap pseudo-AI doll-bots. Bernie Howes stood in the middle of the bustling crowd, slurping his noodles noisily.

"You comin'?" he said. "I ain't got all day."

I turned to wave at Ricky, but he was already busy serving the next customer. As I walked past Howes I muttered under my breath, "You bring any friends?"

"No. . . " He paused with clear broth dripping off his moustache, his eyes scanning the surrounding buildings and the crowd of people. Then he dumped his noodles in the nearest garbage can and said, "Time to go."

We speed-walked through the market, darting between shoppers and avoiding vendors, as Howes led the way toward a standard issue unmarked police boiler in dull grey. He opened the door and we slid inside, and he steered the thing out onto a main grid line. A light rain spattered the windshield.

Howes blew out a lungful of air and loosened the collar on his overcoat. The inside of the boiler was covered in a pale beige leatherette someone had probably once imagined to be classy. The edges of the seats had cracks in them with yellowed foam and dirty white strings showing through. It stank of sweat and stale cigar smoke. An ashtray in the centre console overflowed with stubbed out cigarettes. Howes drummed his fingers against his knees but he didn't take out a stick. I reached into my coat and grabbed a pieces of gum, offered one to him.

He shook his head. "You havin' trouble, Marlowe? Seems you brought a tail to our lunch meeting."

"How's your case against Sammy West looking?" I unwrapped the gum slowly, balled up the wrapper, and tried to balance it on the mountain of stubs. "Because out on the street there's a lot of folks who are acting like an indictment is just a little smoke and mirrors that will blow over in a couple of days."

"The case is solid." He pursed his lips and tugged on the corners of his moustache. He was trying to look thoughtful, but there was anger barely simmering beneath the cool blue surface of his pale eyes. "We've got video testimony from two witnesses and the security footage from Mayor Randall's office. The evidence has been seen, duplicated, and backed up to multiple servers. The smoke and mirrors act is coming from those implicated by West's crime. The evidence isn't the problem."

"Somebody is trying to kill me," I said. "Or worse."

"Or worse?" he said. "What's worse? Even if you ended up dead, too—"

I snapped the gum between my teeth and leaned back in the seat. It creaked in that squeaky way real leather never does. I gave him a hard stare and said, "The other witness is dead?"

He squeezed his eyes shut and cursed under his breath. He said, "Listen, Marlowe. It's been a rough ride, but we're gonna get out of this."

"Somehow I'm not feeling comforted."

"What did you want to see me about, Marlowe?" he said. "I can give you a couple of men if that would make you feel better, but your job is done."

"I was followed to the market," I said. "It's not the first time since I gave my testimony."

"You've just gotta survive the fallout, now."

"Easier said than done, maybe," I said. "But I'm starting to worry it's not my blood they want."

"What are you worried about, then?" He rubbed his hands over is knees. "The press? You're on your own there. Those vultures have their talons into everything."

Dingy lights from the signs of the buildings in the grit and the flickering of rental HoloPop projectors sped past the window as the boiler picked up speed.

I said, "You got any other unexplained dead bodies in the morgue, Howes?"

"This is the Grit District, what do you think?"

"I think there's a body of a woman about my age with a .22 caliber slug in her chest that got picked up near the Spire."

Howes's face paled and he turned his eyes on me with a hard glint in them. "What makes you think that?"

"You can have a smoke if you want," I said. "I won't tell."

Howes cursed and pulled out a crumpled paper package from his coat and drew a thin cigar out of it with his lips. He said, "I'm trying to quit."

"I can see that." I eyed the overflowing ashtray. "Now, you mind telling me if she was killed there? Or was it a drop?"

Howes lit the stick and inhaled deeply. A sheen of sweat shone on his brow. He said, "What the hell are you playing at, Marlowe?"

"Just answer the question," I said. "I have significant skin in this game. I'm trying to help."

"That ain't how it works." His moustache lifted as his top lip curled around the cigar in a snarl. The anger I'd noticed earlier came bubbling to the surface, but his sweat stank like he was afraid. He pointed his finger in my face. "You gave your testimony of your own free will. You weren't coerced. You don't get to hold that over my head for special treatment now."

"The answer might be important to your trial. Because you've got one dead witness and the other one is about to be framed up for murder."

"You?" he shouted, spittle flying from his lips. "You shot Lou Lemon?"

"So you do know about her," I said.

"We had a bulletproof case, goddammit!" He leaned forward and grabbed me by the collars. "If this evidence falls through, Swain is gonna string me up alongside D.A. Fairweather and feed us to the goddamn rats, Marlowe."

I tried not to inhale too deeply of his breath as he stared into my eyes. I said, "I didn't realize you were a religious man."

Bernie Howes's face turned as red as his moustache. He balled up his fists and turned around and hammered the back of his seat. The boiler car rose up over the Grit and the skyline fuzzed behind a mist of rain. The pastel blur of lights made the scene look like a watercolour painting rather than a slum.

I waited for him to finish. Then I said, "So there's no tag out for me yet?"

Howes spun around again, looking like a wrung out dishrag. He wiped his forehead off with the back of his hand, then pulled the cigar out of his mouth. The end sagged and dangled by the paper wrapper where it had snapped in two. He dropped it on the floor of the boiler and pulled out another one, lit it, closed his eyes, and let his head fall back on the seat.

"Did you do it, Marlowe?"

"It was done with a gun that I was carrying earlier last night," I said. "There's footage from security at Cat's Cradle to prove I was carrying one like it. I don't know how good the footage is. But I was slugged in the parking lot and the gun was taken off me then. I found Lou's boiler by the Spire and talked to the desk clerk that night, which will probably also be on camera somewhere, if you can weasel it out of them. Depending on where she was killed, that may or may not help."

"It looks bad." He said, opening his pale blue eyes again. They were ringed with red and had sacks of purple skin hanging off them. "It looks bad enough to make the jury ask questions about your testimony. If they start asking questions about you, the whole case is in a vetchsucking mess. Harding called to gloat about having something on you. I didn't know it was this bad."

"Then I guess I need your help," I said.

"Harding probably knows you're here right now." He stared out the window over my shoulder. "The only reason you ain't dead yet is that he's got a better chance of smearing you while you're still alive. If D.A. Fairweather loses the next election, I might as well have a big red X painted on my forehead if I mess around with you, Marlowe. Fairweather is the only one Swain's afraid of anymore."

I said, "If she convicts Sammy West, she won't lose the election."

Howes took the cigar out of his mouth and blew out through the corner of the bushy red moustache. He said, "Tell me what happened."

I gave him my side of the story, and how I figured Harding played into it all. Fairweather's chief investigator listened with a hard brightness in his eyes and for the first time I could tell that he was a man who was very good at his job. But a good man working in a corrupt system had to work to stay ahead. Bernie Howes, despite his earlier temper tantrum, looked like a man who liked to work.

When I was finished he said, "Why'd the boy toy give you that song and dance about the bump in his apartment, the stiff on the floor? He just lookin' for a laugh?"

"They wanted me to go over there," I said. "They figured I'd go check up on his story, maybe have a look for the planted gun. It got me out of my neck of the woods, too, so they could see if Fairweather had her boys watching my blind side. They got greedy, though, and made a grab for me there. I almost got off clean, but they must have managed to tag the boiler I was in, and tailed me to the hockmarket."

"That's just a guess," Howes said, still sour.

"Sure," I said. "But there's a couple of places we could shake down if we want to do better than guess, if that rates with you."

Howes crushed his cigar in the ashtray and spilled a handful of butts on the floor. He sucked on his teeth and said, "I'd like to get to know some of these mugs who are willing to let go of two mil just to pretty up a fairy-tale."

"I've met them," I said, cracking the knuckles of my flesh hand against the palm of my upgrade. "I don't think you'd like it as much as you think."

He brought up the controls on the centre console and said, "That hack driver of yours is probably just a dirty little crook. But it could be Harding hasn't figured her for a piece in the puzzle. I'd like to bring her in while her memory is still fresh."

"Velma DeLuce," I said and searched her up on my tattler. No listed address anywhere, but she was on the payroll at Busy Bus Party Rentals, just like her ID had said.

I read out the address. Bernie Howes set the heading and the boiler dipped back down onto the street level grid. It made a U-Turn back towards the Grit.

Chapter Thirteen

Busy Bus Party Rentals didn't look like much of a party. The painted sign out front was so peeled and faded that the letters were barely visible. Behind the squalid little office, a stack of portable garage cubes teetered between the two neighbouring buildings looking like a stiff breeze could send the whole pile toppling if it came from the wrong direction. The bottom floor was a wide open workshop with bits and pieces of boilers strewn all over. It looked more like a stripping station for hot vehicles than a legitimate business front.

"I'll wait here," Bernie Howes said, and slid low in the seat. "See if I can spot our tail."

I hunkered down under my hat and trudged out into the rain.

The burly woman at the front counter crossed a muscled pair of arms over her overalls and gave me a look like she'd like to see me stripped and parted out, too. Her eyes lingered a bit too long on my upgrade before finally meeting my gaze. I held up my tattler and showed her a holodoc of my license credentials hoping to give the impression that I was the kind of person who might be missed.

She grunted and said, "Whadda you want?"

"You the dispatcher for Busy Bus?" I asked.

"I can be." She took a dirty toothpick out of the pocket of her overalls and stuck it between a gap in her front teeth. A shock of greenish hair stuck out the bottom of her backward mechanic's hat. She said, "You need a rental?"

"I'm looking for one of your drivers," I said. "A young woman named Velma DeLuce."

She took the toothpick out of her mouth and grinned at me like a dog protecting a slab of meat. She said, "I'll bet you are, sister. What do you want Velma for?"

"I'm a friend of hers," I said.

Somewhere in the background someone dropped a boiler car panel with a loud, echoing clang. A string of curses followed and the woman bellowed over her shoulder, "If you dented that door you'll be workin' it off ya worthless gritsucking pinches."

Then she turned to me and said, "More friends, huh? I always figured Velma for a bit of a loner."

"Yeah," I said. "Me too."

"She works nights." The woman leaned forward on the desk, displaying impressive forearms covered in tattoos like the circuits on a computer chip. She leered at me. "So she ain't in."

"Where can I find her?"

She stared at me for a while like she was trying to peek inside my head. On the big holomap behind her, little blue dots moved around the city, changing to red when they picked up their fares. She said, "Seventeen twenty-three Bethke Street."

"Thanks." I keyed the address into my tattler and found it wasn't too far away. Then I paused. "You remembered that pretty quick. You a friend of hers too?"

"I guess not." The woman looked annoyed. "Couple of other mugs came in asking the same damned—"

I didn't wait for her to finish, I spun on my heel and shoved past an apprentice carrying a crate full of pipe fittings. There was a loud clatter behind me and the woman shouted after me, but I sprinted for the unmarked HCPD boiler waving madly for Howes to open the door.

He kicked it open from the inside and I dove in. He had it moving before I pulled the door closed behind me. I gave him the address and said, "We've been headed. How the hell did Harding find out about her?"

"Harding's probably got scads of low level yes men scanning security cam footage," Howes said. "The man always seems to have something on somebody."

"Half of what he has he sets up himself, it seems."

Howes nodded ruefully. "Sure, but he wouldn't be so damned good at setting his enemies up if he didn't know what they were up to all the time. Probably checks the public security cams and has to narrow it down from there."

"Can't you make this thing go any faster?" I said. My heart thudded in my chest. "Get us on a priority line, for gritssake."

The boiler jumped lines and I felt it increasing speed with a heavy pressure on my chest. Outside, the Grit District sped by like streaks of muddy lights as we raced to beat Heavy Johns hard boy's to Velma DeLuces's place. The woman would be sleeping off her last shift and I doubted there would be security at any kind of complex on Bethke.

Her apartment was in a dead-end cul-de-sac surrounded by defunct warehouse buildings that had been overrun by squatters decades ago. A couple of the buildings had been taken over by more industrious types. While the neighbouring warehouses fell into ruin with scrap metal and bits of recycled plastic filling the windows, sections of concrete crumbling off the corners, and the roof sagging dangerously into the top floor, two of the warehouses had been converted into something resembling apartment buildings, and they managed to run a tight enough door policy people would pay rent on the makeshift suites.

The grid didn't extend onto Bethke, though, and we had to park on the main drag and walk into the warren of abandoned buildings. As we exited the vehicle, a creeping sensation tickled the back of my neck. Scrap cars and plastic tents filled the streets and alleys between the buildings where more squatters had gathered. When it came to living homeless in HoloCity there was safety in numbers. But despite the obvious shanty town set up, there was nobody to be seen.

"You got a piece?" I said under my breath.

Howes' moustache twitched and he scowled at me. "You want to gather a witness statement while carrying a plasma rifle?"

Nothing moved inside the cul-de-sac. The rain spattered down around us, drumming off the top of the abandoned vehicles and sheet of plastic with a percussive rhythm.

"You want to walk through there without one?"

Howes grunted and flipped up a hatch in the floor of the police car. He pulled out a case containing an electric riot gun, smoke grenades, a plasma rifle, and a couple of plasma pistols. He took out one of the pistols and passed it to me. He said, "I'm gonna lose my job for this."

"Better than your life," I said, taking the pistol in my metal hand. "I'll let you do the shooting unless absolutely necessary, that rate? If I don't have to fire they'll never know I had the gat."

He tucked his pistol into a holster inside his coat and slung the rifle over his shoulder. Then we ran across the street and pressed our backs against the crumbling concrete of a warehouse.

At the corner of Bethke and our cross street, two rusted out boilers had a makeshift awning made of scraps of corrugated metal strung up between them like a roof. Ragged blankets and a small solar powered hotplate indicated someone was living there. A doll lay in a puddle between the two cars with most of its hair missing.

"Where is everyone?" Howes said under his breath as we turned the corner on to the cul-de-sac.

Through the drizzle of rain, something flashed in the alley opposite our approach. My gaze darted to the shadows. A pale crescent of light reflected off the shiny surface of a brand new boiler car. I elbowed Howes in the ribs and pointed to it with my chin. "Harding's men know how to clear a room when they need to get to work."

A clatter echoed off the surrounding buildings and Howes whipped the rifle over his shoulder in a flash. An angry yowl cut through the silence and a streak of orange and white shot past us as a scraggly tom cat shot into the street, its bent tail bristled. Howes pressed his lips together, sucking the ruddy hairs of his moustache into his mouth. His pale blue eyes cut across the cul-de-sac like a razor blade. He motioned with his head for us to proceed.

As we turned the corner, the crack of a rifle rent the air, followed by a pained shout and a stream of cursing. Howes and I dove behind the rusted boilers and I peeked out from behind a busted out window. There was another crack, and I ducked my head.

"That's no pea-shooter," I hissed.

The whine of a plasma weapon spooling up came from the far end of the street, and Howes used the sound as cover to get his own weapon ready. He said, "We have to get closer. I'll cover you."

I planned my trajectory and crouched low to the ground, my heart thudding in my ears. A burst of blue-white plasma bolts exploded from behind a sheet of pink plastic siding leaned up against one of the apartment buildings. I ran for the next cover, staying as close to the ground as I could. Sparks flew as two more cracks of return fire pinged off the metal of the abandoned car next to the pink plastic.

Howes slung the rifle over his back and scuttled over to my hiding spot. I pointed to the sheet of plastic. "They're over there. Someone's shooting at them from the second floor of the brown brick building, right above the sign."

Howes pulled out a pair of tactical lenses, slid them over his eyes, and leaned around the corner of the upturned garbage bin we'd hidden ourselves behind. He said, "There's two men. Big guys. One's down, not moving. The other one's hit in the shoulder, but he's still locked and loaded. The other shooter is a young woman, dark hair—"

"That's Velma," I said, grinning. "I guess they didn't get the jump on her after all."

"I can tag the other guy from here but I don't want her getting' the wrong idea," Howes said.

"Gimme a second," I said. I set down my pistol and flipped through my tattler until I found a reel advert for Otto's Curried Potato. "Which way is the goon facing? Us or her?"

"Her," Howes said, his voice tight. "Looks like he's getting ready to take another shot. I need to move."

I flicked on the holoprojector on my tattler and shone the ad for curried potatoes into the rain over my head. Howes raised his eyebrows at me. I said, "Go, she'll know what it means."

"And if she doesn't?"

"I've got a hook-up for rigs to replace anything he blows off of you." I held my tattler up and shifted my weight so I could aim my pistol around the edge of the metal bin. "I can hit him from here if I have to, just stay to the right."

Howes nodded and closed his eyes. He blew out his cheeks slowly like he was counting in his head, then he broke and ran. He stayed low, his trench coat dragging in the puddles behind him, and sidled toward the buildings on the perimeter. When the goon lifted his plasma rifle to take another shot at Velma, Howes dove for partial cover, spun, and planted a bead between the guy's shoulder blades.

"HCPD," he shouted. "Drop your weapon and get on the ground."

The goon let the rifle fall to his side and turned around slowly. But he didn't let go of it and he didn't drop to the ground. Blood had soaked through the crisp grey suit on his left shoulder, and he kept his arm tucked in close to his body like there might be a wound in his belly, too, He cocked his head and tsk-tsked at Howes like the detective was the one having a bad day. The goon curled a lip and said, "You ain't supposed to be here."

"Get on the ground!"

I could hear the whine of Howe's weapon as he prepared to take the shot. I hoped he wasn't going to use this as an opportunity to show how to play by the book. The goon stepped forward, grinning wickedly. He said, "Why don't you show me how."

The hand he'd tucked against his belly whipped out. A silver pistol glinted in his thick fist like the shiny toy gun for a robot soldier. Howes flinched back.

"Get down, Howes!" I shouted. "He's got a laser!"

Howes flinched behind the sheet of metal and rolled. A red beam hit the spot he'd been standing with an explosion of rubble. I tightened my finger on the trigger of my plasma pistol and took a deep stabilizing breath.

Before I could take the shot, another crack split the air. The goon's forehead split open like an overripe melon. He stood there for a moment, his arms twitching at his sides, and he fell face first into a greasy puddle oozing out from beneath one of the abandoned cars. Or, it would have been face first if he'd had any face left.

I killed the hologram and stood up tentatively, peering over the edge of the upturned garbage bin. "Velma," I called out. "Is that you?"

"It's me," she said. "Is your friend down?"

Howes shook his head and gave me a thumbs up. I said, "He's okay. You got both of those hard boys. We good to come out?"

"That depends," she said, her voice still tight with adrenaline. "What do you want with me?"

The busted out windows of the surrounding windows began to fill with faces. I said, "Can we talk about it in private?"

She paused. "I thought you weren't working with the cops no more."

"Special circumstances," I said. "And I brought Howes here to offer you a bit of protection. Looks like you didn't need it."

She didn't answer. The window above the sign of the brown brick building was empty. The sign below it read PARADISE PLACE. Howes swung his rifle back over his shoulder and drew his pistol. He stepped out of his hiding spot and approached the bodies with his tattler cam scanning the scene.

He kicked the laser pistol out of the dead man's fingers. "Marlowe, I need a hand here."

I advanced cautiously, aware of all the eyes on us. I said, "You sure you want me in on this? I'm not an official consultant on this case."

"I can arrange that," Howes said. "I need you to hold the camera."

He detached a mobile recording unit from his tattler and passed it over to me. I said, "Swain is going to choke on his own bile if you put me back on the HCPD payroll."

"We'll let Fairweather deliver the news," he grinned at me. "After she wins the next election."

I shrugged and held the recording unit steady while Howes rifled through the pockets of the dead man and spoke into the camera.

"This is Chief Investigator Bernie Howes on the location of a gang shooting on Bethke Street," he said. "I've got an illegal Class 2 Laser pistol here in the possession of an Antoni Wójcik—" He flashed the ID card at the camera. "—registered as a bodyguard to Biz District board director, John Harding. The weapon appears to be marked as a product of the Eastern Sprawl, serial number—" He rattled off a long series of letters and numbers. Then he motioned me to follow him over to other body and gave him the same treatment. "Here we have Pole Ackerman, convicted felon and member of the Red Line gang. Released from custody a three days ago, just couldn't wait to get back into the thick stuff."

"That's not the guy who knocked me down at Cimarro's," I said. "But it's the guy I was looking at when I got knocked down. If boy Valiant was telling a sliver of truth this morning, that's the guy who shot Lou Lemon."

"That wouldn't shock me," Howes said, pulling out the rest of the goon's arsenal and motioning for me to get it all on video.

A door opened at the bottom of the brown brick building and Velma DeLuce leaned against the doorframe, looking pale and tired. Her skin had turned a bit green around her cleft lip.

"You think you can keep these creeps off of my doorstep," she said, "I'd be willing to give a statement."

Howes took the camera from me and slid it back into the slot on his tattler. He said, "You better go lay down, sister. If I'm any judge of colour, you're gonna paint the sidewalk with your breakfast."

Chapter Fourteen

V ELMA'S APARTMENT WAS CLEAN and simple. She didn't have a lot, but she made do with what she had. A single cot squatted in the corner of a small living area. Thin brown curtains hung over a barred window. The floor was covered in something that might have been a carpet once, but which had been worn down to a crosshatching of twine-like threads that stuck to the bottoms of my boots as I shuffled awkwardly at the door.

A black-haired boy with huge round eyes peered at me from around a divider made of plastic crates and colourful scraps of fabric. Velma sat on the edge of the bed with her head between her knees and an ancient carbine rifle with a scratched and dented wooden stock. A box of cartridges lay underneath the window next to a sprinkle of crushed glass from where the hack driver must have punched the barrel of the rifle through in order to have a clean shot at Harding's men.

"It was what they said about Pietre," Velma DeLuce said from between her knees. "That's what cracked me. They said they'd come back and get him if I didn't play their game."

She blew out a long breath and lifted her gaze to face me. She said, "I left you at the Spire. I thought you were trouble. I didn't know I'd already gotten myself into it by making that deal with the highbinder vetch and her twist."

"Okay, Ms. DeLuce," Howes said slowly. He crouched down in front of her with the camera pointed at her. "Let's have it from the start."

I leaned up against the doorframe and crossed my arms. The kid wrinkled his nose at me. I stuck out my tongue and he ducked behind the wall of crates, giggling.

"I was just getting up, making something for us to eat," Velma said carefully. "I have to work the night shift and Gela, the lady down the hall who watches Pietre when I'm away, she doesn't like to have to feed him before bed. I was in the kitchen when someone knocked on the door. I figured it was Gela, and got the boy to answer it. These two thugs come in, push him down on the ground. Pietre tried to run away but the lanky one grabbed him and made him stay. The fat guy sat on the bed there and made me tell him all about last night—twice. Then he said I was to forget I'd met anybody or come into the BizDiz with anybody. The rest was silky."

Howes nodded and said, "And when did you first see this woman here?"

"I didn't notice the time," Velma said. "Maybe eleven-thirty? I checked in at the office at about one-thirty, when I dropped off my hack. We were in the curry shop for about half an hour."

"So, say midnight when you met her?"

Velma rubbed a hand over her scarred lip and shook her head. "The owner of the curry place told me he closed up at midnight. He wasn't closing when we left. Must have been earlier."

Howes glowered at me over his moustache and I shrugged. "I don't remember," I said. "But the curry shop has a camera I bet even Harding doesn't know about. If you ask him nice I bet you could get the feed."

"Okay," Howes said. "Tell us the rest about these hard boys you put holes into."

"The skinny guy said I probably wouldn't have to talk to anybody about it. If I did and I talked right they'd leave me cushy. If I talked wrong, they'd be back for my boy."

"Harding's got his fingers into the Red Zone," I said. "They like 'em young."

Velma gritted her teeth and the tendons stood out on the side of her neck. She said, "They went away. I waited for them to get outside and it was like something in my brain was tearing itself apart. Everyone had taken off when they saw these mugs come in. No one was in my way. I figured even if I did what they said, they'd wanna wring me out for more. When I saw you two pull up I thought they'd called in reinforcements. I got mad."

Howes made some official statements for the sake of the video then turned off the recording. He said, "You might have to come down to the station with us. Can your neighbour watch your boy?"

"I'll get sacked if I miss a shift," she said. "Busy doesn't like flakes."

"That's the green haired broad at the garage?" I said.

Velma nodded.

"Something tells me she won't mind a driver with a little guts," I said. "I can talk to her."

Velma called down the hall and a short, round woman with a pleasant face scuttled out of one of the neighbouring apartments to scoop up the dark haired boy. She and Velma spoke to one another in a dialect I didn't recognize and Velma grabbed a rain coat out of the closet. I stepped into the hallway after her and Howes grabbed my sleeve.

"She don't know about Lou being dead," he said. "No need to bring it up yet."

I nodded and closed the door behind us. When we got downstairs, the flashing lights of two HCPD squad cars greeted us. Howes got Velma squared away with one of his men and left them to the clean up.

As we walked back to his car, Howes said, "Well?"

I said, "The killers knew about the hack switch, and the boy friend reached town with the cush. So I can't figure this being Cimarro's job. She's not the kind of girl to let anybody play around with her two million creds. Valiant was in on the kill, and it was done for a reason."

Howes opened the door of his boiler and grinned mirthlessly at me. He said, "Sure, it was done so you could be framed for it."

"It's an ugly world when some folks take so little account of a human life—or two million creds. Lou was bumped off so I could be framed and the cush was passed to me to make the frame tighter."

"Maybe they thought they could roll you," Howes said. "Two mil is nothing to sneeze at."

I pulled out a piece of chewing gum and held it in my fingers. "That would be a little too dumb, even for me. What do we do now? Swain's not going to like your evidence with me hanging around the edges."

Howes got into the car. "I can hold it back for a day or two. That hack driver would rather not sing too loud about it. We just gotta hang onto it until the trial is over."

"I'd like it that way too," I said. "The less said about me the better. I guess you can't hold it down for long, but you might hold it down long enough for me to see a big boy about a fluffy white dog."

"You been on the street too long, Marlowe," Howes said, lighting up another cigar. "I don't understand half the gritsucking words that come out of your face."

"Don't worry about it," I said. "You've got your hands full."

I had him drop me off at my office.

Chapter Fifteen

I HAD JUST OPENED the door when my tattler pinged, a voice message from an unknown caller. I transferred the incoming message to the holophone on my desk, hung up my coat, and grabbed a can of NRG out of the mini-fridge. I flipped open the lid on the box of Kreme Kween doughnuts Dickie had brought that morning—was it only this morning?—and bit into a somewhat sodden but still delicious piece of candied carbohydrates.

The message played while I chewed. It was a garbled assortment of audio clips mixed by one of those apps favoured by punk kids pranking their friends and serial killers leaving cryptic messages for the police. This one was inviting me to a special dinner at the Casa de Néon, a highbinder joint in the Biz District that I'd never be allowed inside under normal circumstances. It was lovingly signed off by J.H.

I finished off the NRG and licked my fingers clean of the bits of pink icing. If Heavy John Harding was inviting me to a business meeting at the

Casa de Néon, that meant he thought he had a reason for me to do business with him. That meant, he was going to offer me protection against Chief Swain. That, or he'd thought of another way to tighten the noose around my neck.

I decided I should test the waters. I ignored the burner number the message had been sent from and pinged Harding's business line. I kept the holofeed off. I wasn't in a hurry to see the big boy before I had to.

First I got a receptionist. Then I got a nervous man who sounded like he thought Heavy John's name might blow up in his mouth. Then I got Harding himself.

"Marlowe," he said. "I'm glad you called. I have been thinking about our talk this afternoon and I have a better proposition for you. Come to dinner tonight... and you might bring along that cush. You should have enough time to get it out of the bank."

"It's not your money," I said.

He chuckled, a thin and brittle sound over the tinny speaker on my tattler. "Don't be foolish. Those credits are all marked, and I wouldn't want to have to accuse you of stealing."

I considered that and decided I didn't believe it. I tossed my can into the recycling chute and said, "I might be willing to turn it over to the party that I got it from—in your presence."

"I told you, that party left town," he said. There was a muffled sound as he covered the mic on his comm. Then he came back and said, "I'll see what I can do. No tricks, please. I'll send a car for you."

"Of course," I said. "No tricks."

We hung up and I scanned the feedreels for news on the shooting of Lou Lemon. Still no one talking about it. Not even an anonymous tip in the gossip reels. Someone was sitting on it, but I couldn't figure why. Even Harding didn't cover that much ground. I called Howes and couldn't reach him, but I left him a message anyway. Once I couldn't procrastinate anymore, I went down to see about my ride.

The boiler arrived promptly, a sleek red pod on full auto. Even the windows were tinted to match the shimmering cherry finish of the body paint. It was the kind of car that turned heads in the Grit and a few people stopped to stare as a thin white beam of light extended from the security dome on the top of the pod. It scanned the area, then focussed on my face, zipping back and forth like a 3D printer taking my measurements. I hoped Harding wouldn't sell my image to the sex bot industry as revenge after tonight.

A circular door dilated open to allow me inside, and I slid in, my cargo pants sliding against the buttery smooth black leather seats. An expensive light diffuser swirled above my head, casting psychedelic dreamscapes of colour over the interior of the pod. When the door closed and the boiler moved back onto the main grid, a pedestal rose up from the floor containing a bottle of expensive gin and a pair of crystal glasses. Liquid smoke poured out of the container from the pellets of dry ice packed into the bottom. I ground my teeth together. Either Heavy John Harding was trying to get a dig in about my drinking problem, or he had sent his pimp-mobile because he thought I'd be impressed.

The boiler's route had been preprogrammed. There was nothing I could do now but wait and hope Harding really did want to meet me at Casa de Néon and he wasn't about to deliver me into the hands of an underground organ harvesting ring in order to get rid of me. I tried to send a message to Dickie just in case, but the boiler had a comms blocker installed. How romantic. The muscles in my stomach tightened.

No, unless Harding could secure his frame-up he needed me alive. If I went missing after giving a testimony like I had, it would only serve to prove Sammy West had friends on the outside and further implicate the crooked board members. Harding needed me alive, and he needed to be able to call me a liar. It wouldn't surprise me at all if he had kept Swain off my back while he set his scene.

I leaned back in the seat and tried to relax as the boiler took me deeper into the Biz District than I had any business being. I'd seen reel footage of Casa de Néon before, a low glass building—the very lack of additional floors an extravagance in the outrageously expensive BizDiz—shaped like a crystalline fortress. I'd written it off as the typical highbinder aesthetic, gauche and gimmicky. But as the boiler pulled up to Casa de Néon in all its iridescent glory I had to admit it made an impression.

Coloured lights glittered through the glass panels, reflecting and refracting off of one another in an otherworldly dreaminess. The door dilated open and I clumsily exited the vehicle. My good-enough-for-the-Grit look didn't translate so well here. I strode up to the front door like a sooty smudge coming to stain the party linens.

Harding's man, Seb, greeted me at the door, dressed in a suit that looked like it had been sewn out of the white plastic they used to wrap up construction sites. The inventiveness of the fashion sect never ceased to amaze. Still, he looked more the part than I did. He grinned at me like we were old pals, and led me inside the building without saying a word.

Inside, the restaurant was empty except for a large frosted glass table in the middle of the room, shaped like a stretched out ellipse and scattered with geometric flowers made of blown glass, and three smaller round tables arranged around it like handmaidens to the queen.

Heavy John Harding, all dolled up in a suit of virginal linen, sat at the centre of the large table with a silver domed serving dish in front of him. The little white dog had one leg stretched up over its head, like a cat, while it licked at its genitals on the table next to its owner. Fiver Valiant, in a matching suit, sat at one of the smaller tables. Seb deposited me in front of the middle one and then positioned himself at the edge of the room, a silent observer. The third table remained unoccupied.

Harding clapped his hands together and a parade of skeletally thin servers dressed in pearly white latex swept in on teetering heels. One of the androgynous figures pulled out a chair for me, and poured water into a tall crystal glass. They set a smaller domed dish in front of me. Then, in a swift, synchronized motion, the servers lifted the domes from our plates and flowed back out of the room like atoms on a slipstream.

A thick slab of meat sat in the middle of my plate, along with a dash of greenery that was too exotic for me to identify, and a tiny cake of starchy white stuff that could have once been a potato. It smelled like it might cause my bank account to collapse upon itself and start vacuuming up holocreds like black hole. I didn't pick up my fork.

"Well, Marlowe," Heavy John Harding boomed across the room at me, his little white teeth flashing in his massive face. "What do you think of the highlife? Think you can get used to it?"

"A person has to be careful not to sneeze in a place like this," I said. "One wrong move and it might all come down on his head."

"Or hers," Harding said, still grinning.

Valiant shrugged his narrow shoulders and poked at the meat with his knife as if unwilling to believe it was real. He looked the way a kid looks on his birthday when he gets the toy advertised on the feedreels and realizes that it isn't quite as glamorous as it looked on the holoscreen. We all drank from our glasses and looked very solemn.

"We're all here but two," I said. "Is that enough for a quorum?"

Harding's head tilted so sharply I was afraid his right jowl might fall off. He said, "What's that supposed to mean?"

"Lou Lemon is in the morgue," I said. "And Ms. Cimarro is dodging cops, presumably, if she's worried at all. Otherwise we're all here. All the interested parties."

Valiant flinched as if someone had smacked his face. Then his muscles seemed to melt and he sank lower in his chair.

Harding picked up his fork and knife and cut into the meat. Blood spurted out of it, the only real colour in the room if you didn't count the unidentifiable vegetables. He took a bite and chewed slowly, then he folded his fingers on the table in front of him and licked his lips.

"The cush," he said coldly. "I'll take charge of it now."

"Not now or any other time," I said. A puddle of blood oozed out of the meat on my plate, too. "I didn't bring it."

Harding didn't move, but his jowls quivered and his cheekbones glowed a violent shade of red. I glanced at Seb at the side of the room. He had his hands in his pockets and a toothpick in his mouth. His eyes looked half asleep. He didn't look too worried about Harding's health.

The big boy spoke softly, like his words were padded in the finest silk, "Holding out, are you, Marlowe?"

"That rates, don't it?" I gave him a charming smile, as near as I could make one. "While I have it I'm fairly safe. You overplayed your hand when you let me get my dirty Grit skid fingers on it. I'd be a fool not to hold onto the advantage."

Harding laughed, a sound like an old engine backfiring, and he shoved another piece of dripping meat into his mouth. "Safe?" He chewed violently.

"Maybe not from a frame-up," I said. "But the last one didn't stick on me... Not from being zapped in a back alley, either. But that'll be harder next time too... Fairly safe from being shot in the back and having you sue my estate for the cush, though. That's safe enough for now."

Harding scratched the pooch behind the ears and pressed his thick lips together.

"We need to get a few things straightened out tonight," I said. "Like who takes the rap for Lou Lemon?"

"What makes you think you don't?" he snarled.

"I gave my alibi a spit-shine," I said. "I didn't know how good it was until I did a little digging. I'm clear now, regardless of who turns in what gun with what story. The hard boys you sent to bust up my alibi got a little busted up themselves."

Harding said, "Is that right?"

"Couple of gentleman named Antoni Wójcik and Pole Ackerman," I said. "They're both very dead. The law has them now, and everything they were carrying. Including illegal weapons from the Sprawl and an ID card naming you as an employer. Hope that doesn't upset you too much."

"Certainly not," Harding said, growling under his breath. "It's an obvious set up. Cimarro, probably. She's the one who had Lemon killed."

"Is that your new idea?" I stuck my fork in the top of the meat and let it stand there, a spire of silver built on dead flesh. "I think it stinks."

Valiant turned his wan visage toward me and said, his voice trembling, "Of course—of course it was Cimarro who had Lou killed... I told you it was her men that did it."

"You did tell me that," I said. "Doesn't mean it makes any sense. What would she do that for, a case of cush she never got back? They wouldn't have killed her at your apartment. They'd have dragged you both back to Cimarro until you told her exactly where you'd left it. You arranged for that kill, Fiver, and the stunt with the hack driver that was meant to sidetrack me—baby wants what baby gets, isn't that right?—it had nothing to do with fooling Cimarro's boys."

He put up a hand to his mouth, his eyes glittering beneath sloppily painted eyelids.

"It took me a little too long to clue in," I went on. "But I didn't figure on anything quite as tangled up as this mess. Cimarro had no motive to put the lead into Lou, unless it got back the money she'd been cheated out of. Supposing she learned about the scam that quickly, which is fast even for a dame like Miss Candy."

Harding cut into his meat. He kept cutting long after the blade had begun to grind against the plate. Valiant shifted in his seat as if it was a bed of nails. Miserably, he said, "Lou knew all about the play. She planned it with Ainslo, the croupier with the white eyes. Ainslo wanted some cush to make a getaway, wanted to move out to the Sprawl.

Cimarro would have gotten wise eventually. But not too soon, if I hadn't gotten so hot at the wheel. I was too noisy, drew too much attention. It was me who got Lou killed, just not the way you mean."

I sipped from my water glass and swished it around my mouth a little. Then I swallowed and said, "Silky. Cimarro takes the wrap. I don't have a problem with that."

Harding and Valiant relaxed like someone had pulled the plug out of a couple of mismatched inflatable sex dolls.

"Where was Lou going to be when Cimarro was supposed to find out she'd gotten jammed?"

"Gone," Valiant said. "Long gone. And I was going to be gone with her."

"It's a nice enough story," I said. "Except that I know why Lou was killed."

Seb roused himself with a light stretch and touched something on his hip. "This broad giving you a hard time, chief?"

Harding waved him away, his eyes shining like tiny beads in his fat face. "Let her rant."

I shifted in my chair so that I had both Seb and Harding in my peripheral vision. Outside, the sky was darkening, and the glass walls of the restaurant seemed to brighten in their light display. Rain was coming down. There was no one in the room but us, and the strange coloured shadows cast by the crystalline walls seemed to edge closer to us, forcing us closer together.

Harding reached into his coat, and I tensed. He pulled out his glass pipe and lit it with a hollowed out expression. He spoke slowly, like the words were coming from deep inside and were hard to get out. "Forget all of this. Let's make a deal about the cush... Sammy West hung himself in his cell this afternoon."

Valiant lurched in his chair and winced, wrapping his arms over his belly. He wore a red mesh shirt beneath the white jacket that didn't seem to keep him very warm.

"Did he have any help?" I said.

A flash of movement at the edge of my vision made me whip around. Seb jumped at my movement and hit me with a stern look. But I wasn't looking at Seb. Someone else was in the room with us.

A hollow pop echoed off the slanted sheets of glass in the entryway, making the building hum like a crystal glass struck to make a toast. The ringing rose in pitch until it became an itch in my eardrums. Seb frowned, a little red flower blooming over the pocket of his slick white jacket. Then he fell forward and landed with his arms folded beneath him and his face flat on the floor. A fizz of pinkish fluid sprayed the wall behind him like graffiti.

The sharp click of spiked heels on a hard surface announced our missing dinner guest. Candy Cimarro, dressed in a pantsuit that seemed to be made of the rainbows floating on top of an oil slick, slunk into the room with a silenced, long barrelled pistol clutched in her fingers.

"Don't move," she purred. "I'm a fair shot—even with a few too many stims in me."

Her face was so pale she might have been transparent. Maybe that's how she'd hidden in the entry way. She said, "I do love Casa de Néon. Such a pretty place to get high. Sound carries quiet well, too."

Harding dropped his hands beneath the table and Miss Candy cocked her ice blonde head in his direction. "You should have an alarm," she said. "Men like you always do. I'd advise against using it. If any of those doors open, even a server delivering drinks, I'll let the light into that fat skull of yours."

Harding dropped his pipe and gathered up what bluster he could find with short notice. He said, "What do you want?"

She strode past me and said, "I knew you were a dick."

I didn't say anything.

Candy pointed the gun at Harding and smiled her imitation smile. "I've been bled by your organization for years. But this is too much. I don't mind being cheated out of the money so much. It's trivial in the long run. Now I'm wanted for the murder of this Lemon dame. And now some pinch has been made to confess that he overheard me sending in my boys... It's too far, Harding. You're getting too big."

Harding's jowls trembled and his little teeth glinted. He folded his hands in front of him and tried not to shake. The fluffy white dog lapped at the blood on his plate.

"I would like to get the cush back," Candy Cimarro drawled lazily. "I would like to get clear of this rap. But more than anything I'd like for you to speak so that I can shoot one of your undersized teeth out of your oversized mouth."

Seb stirred on the ground, slipping in the puddle of blood that spread across the floor. Harding's gaze had frozen upon a spot in front of his face as he used everything in his power not to look at his bodyguard.

"Ainslo talked to me." The gambling queen shook her head and her pale blond curls bounced over her shoulders. "I made sure of that. You killed Lou Lemon because she was a secret witness against Sammy West. The D.A. managed to keep the secret. I'd bet that two mil wad that this dick here managed to keep it, once she figured it out. But poor Lou couldn't keep it. She told her boy toy. And the boy told you... so you came up with this neat little plan."

Her words hung in the air and buzzed off the glass decorations until I thought I'd go insane with the sound of not-quite silence.

"You made the suggestion to Ainslo," she said. "Didn't you? You fixed him up, and he fixed up Lou. It wasn't hard to pull over on me because I don't play my wheels crooked. I don't expect my croupiers to bet against the house."

The shoulders of Harding's suit seemed to vibrate. His round face had paled until it was like a stained white mask. Seb had propped himself up on one elbow now. His eyes were barely open, but he had a snub-nosed plasma cannon gripped in his bloody fingers.

"Never bet against the house, Harding." Cimarro leaned forward, her thin lips curling at the edges into something less like a smile and more like a feral snarl. Her pale finger tightened on the trigger at the same time that Seb's gun pulsed. An explosion of sound shook the building.

Cimarro grunted and arched her back, twisting as she fell, sprawling over the glassy white floor. Seb dropped his gun and collapsed on his back, his chest rising and falling fitfully.

I stood and moved quickly across the room and kicked Cimarro's rod underneath the big table. Doing this, I saw that she'd gotten off one shot, at least. Heavy John Harding wore a dinner bib of bright red blood pouring over his crisp white jacket from a hole in his fleshy throat. His little white dog whined and pawed at his chest.

I strode over to Seb and checked his pulse. There was a mess of blood around him, but his ticker was still ticking. A door opened next to me and one of the androgynous servers stared out at the room in stunned silence. "Is there a problem?" she said.

I almost laughed.

"We're taking care of it," I said. "Keep the rest of the staff out."

She nodded and closed the door. I had to wonder about the kinds of thing you got used to working in a place like this.

Fiver Valiant got to his feet, his gaze wavering around the room like he was seeing things that weren't there. Maybe he was. Maybe he just thought he was. When he spoke, his words were made of glass, as cold and fragile as the room itself. He said, "I didn't know they were going to kill Lou. But even if I'd wanted to I couldn't have done anything about it. They laid into me with a branding iron just to give me a taste of what I'd get. Look!"

He pulled open the jacket and lifted the mesh shirt. Angry red welts striped his torso like a mockery of his strappy red outfit from last night.

"You need to get that looked at, brother," I said, remembering the way he'd flinched and winced when he'd visited me in the office. I'd taken his glassy eyed stare for a bad come down, not blistered skin. "I'm going to have to call the police for this, though. And a medic for Seb."

I lifted my tattler to make the call and he stumbled toward me, gripping my upgrade in his thin hands. His voice tumbled out of him like water rushing over stones, cold and trembling, but unstoppable. "I thought they'd just hold her until after the trial. But they dragged her out of that hack and shot her without saying a word. Then the skinny one took the hack up to the Spire and the stocky one brought me to some shack in the Red Zone. Harding was there. He explained how the frame-up was going to work. He promised me the cush if I did what he said. Then he did his demonstration for what I'd get if I didn't. He laughed as he did it."

I pulled out of his grip hand said, "I'm sorry, but I've gotta make the call. My skin is on the line here too."

"Listen to me!" Valiant's voice rose an octave or two and did a little dance in the back of his throat. "Harding set the frame up with Ainslo. He was one

of the gang that arranged for Mayor Randall takin'
that hit. I didn't—"

"Sure, Fiver," I said. "It's silky. Take it easy."

We stood there in silence until the glass stopped
humming. I felt as if there might be a lot of people
outside the doors, crouched down and listening.
Still, I said, "Harding had it set up pretty well. It
could have worked. But he got cocky, his plan got
too big, too elaborate. It would have put us both
out as witnesses, if Lou got killed and I got framed
up for killing her. They could make it look like two
conspirators turning against one another. But that
kind of thing, too many people, it always sort of
blows up in your face."

"Lou just wanted to get out of HoloCity." Tears
ran down the young man's cheeks. He twisted his
fingers in the suit jacket. "She was scared. She
thought the roulette trick was a pay-off, her ticket
out."

"Yeah," I said. "It was her ticket all right."

I turned my back on the kid and punched in
an emergency call to the HCPD. When a tired
sounding dispatcher picked up I said, "I'd like to
report a murder at the Casa de Néon. Persons of
significance are involved."

There were some shuffling noises from the other
side of the door and I heard footsteps running, dull
sounds from the next room over. I looked over my
shoulder and Valiant was gone. I didn't bother to
go after him.

Instead I figured I'd get a jump on the media
machine and I pinged Ruby Blue at the BizDiz

News reel—I'd always kind of liked her—and gave her my side of the story.

I didn't have too much trouble. Fairweather pulled more weight around town than I realized. Even Chief Swain was scared to look my way until the buzz died down.

They picked up Ainslo on the slug train heading out to the suburbs. He broke and implicated five other members of the Red Line gang. Swain took his frustration out on them instead.

Fiver Valiant made a clean get away. I never heard from him again.

Oh, and the two mil?

Howes came and collected it from me. He let me keep a two grand fee, which was better than I usually made even considering the number of times I got knocked down. I can't complain.

He retired from the force before Fairweather came up for re-election, though. Makes a person wonder what he did with all that cush.

Or maybe that's just me, being a dick.

THE END

Glossary

T HE FOLLOWING ARE SOME of the slang words I've used in the Bubbles in Space and HoloCity Case Files series. Where applicable, I have indicated the original meanings of these words from classic pulp novels. Did I miss any? Please let me know if you'd like a term added to the list! Send me a message at contact@scjensen.com

Bangtail – space shuttles, originally "racehorse"

Boiler – both personal and rental maglev vehicles, originally "car"

Button man—hit man, hired killer, original meaning

CBI—Computer Brain Interface

Cush – money (a cushion, something to fall back on), original meaning

Dizzy – crazy or foolish, originally "to be ga-ga for"

Drift – get lost, original meaning

Fade – to kill, originally "go away" or "get lost"

Feedcasters – live video jockeys on social media

Feedreels – live video footage covering news, social events, gossip, and entertainment topics

Glow-up – originally "a glow" was to be drunk, here used as a drug-induced high

'Gram – hologram image or video

Grid – a network, can refer to the electromagnetic transportation grid the boilers run on, or a communication network

Hack – a taxi, original meaning

Highbinder – a corrupt official, original meaning

Kiss – to punch, original meaning

Kretek – clove cigarettes, original meaning

Long bird – sky train

Pinch – a drug addict, originally "to arrest"

Plug – an android

Pro skirt – a prostitute, original meaning

Rate – used to indicate veracity or quality. "That rates" may mean either "That's good" or "That sounds true," originally "to be good" or "to count for something"

Scatter – a hideout, or to hide, original meaning

Shill – an accomplice of a hawker, gambler, or swindler who acts as an enthusiastic customer to entice or encourage others, original meaning

Silk – good/okay, original meaning

Skin – a nanoparticle "shell" used to change one's appearance, often used for robots, androids, and personal enhancement for those who can afford it

Slug – subway

Tattler – a communication device similar to a smartphone

Ticket – a license, original meaning

Top – to kill

Twist – a romantic partner, original meaning (female only)

Upgrade – a cybernetic replacement part

Vetch – derogatory term for females and femmes

Author's Note

THANKS FOR READING HOLOCITY Hard Boys. I hope you enjoyed your time with Bubbles and the gang! This is the second novella I've written in the HoloCity Case Files, a companion series to Bubbles in Space.

The stories in HoloCity Case Files are all inspired by Raymond Chandler's short stories featuring the iconic 1930s hard-boiled detective, Philip Marlowe. I've had a lot of fun re-imagining them and re-interpreting them with my own settings and characters.

If you had fun, too, please drop me a quick review! It helps other readers find books they will love, and it will put a twinkle in my eye. Reviews are the absolute best thing you can do to support indie authors. Well, besides buying our books, that is!

If you'd like to be the first to know about new releases and giveaways, or want to become a member of my advance review team, please join my VIP Reader's Club!

I can't wait to meet you <3

Want more Bubbles Marlowe?

The adventures continue in two exciting series by
S.C. Jensen.
HoloCity Case Files

Dames for Hire

HoloCity Hard Boys

Neon Goldfish
Bubbles in Space

Tropical Punch

Chew 'Em Up

Pop 'Em One

Spit 'Em Out

Cherry Bomb

Join Bubbles Marlowe on her first detective cases in...

HoloCity Case Files

A series of standalone cyber-noir mystery novellas inspired by Raymond Chandler's 'Philip Marlowe' short stories.

Complete Series
now available!

Bubbles in Space is
"...gritty and glamorous,
violent and dazzling..."

Welcome to Undercity:

An exciting new series from S.C. Jensen

I'M NOT DEAD YET, but this isn't living...

They call me the Ghost. I wander the surface of this nameless city, unseen, searching for the sister I lost many years ago. It is a forsaken place, its battle-scarred surface left to burn under a relentless sun.

I should have given up. But when I uncover a disturbing connection between Lyca's disappearance and the ancient wars that destroyed our city, I refuse to let it go.

The city is restless. Long-forgotten wounds are beginning to itch. People whisper about rebellion, rising-up to take back what was stolen from us. I only want what was stolen from me.

I would do anything to find my sister, even if it means starting a war. But some secrets were meant to stay hidden, and what I have uncovered will change the city and its people forever.

I'm not dead yet, but I will be soon...

Undercity – Timekeepers' War

ABOUT THE SERIES:

In a world scorched by natural disaster, and a city destroyed by centuries of war, hope is a word most people have forgotten. Mutant soldiers enforce the rule of the few, monsters lurk in the tunnels below ground, and an enigmatic group called the Timekeepers play a deadly game with the lives of the survivors...

When one woman stands up to fight, she finds an army behind her. And when she falls, she'll take an empire down.

For fans of Leigh Bardugo's Six of Crows, Scott Lynch's Lies of Locke Lamora, and Margaret Atwood's Oryx and Crake. This dystopian science-fantasy series will keep you guessing with secrets, simmering tension, and high-stakes action.

THEY THOUGHT WE WERE BEATEN.
THEY THOUGHT WE WERE WEAK.
THEY THOUGHT WRONG.

**Available
April 11, 2022**